## AUTHOR'S NOTE

My regular readers will know that I often insert characters that have appeared in previous stories in my books and have done so in Virgin. Though this book can be read as a stand-alone your reading pleasure may be enhanced by reading the Crystal Jake Complete Eden series.

For all those readers who are not familiar with the Eden family, I've Included book one of this series so you can get acquainted with this bad boy, Jake Eden and I've furthermore included an additional story, Sexy Beast which follows on from The Crystal Jake, complete Eden series and is book one of the Bad Boys of London Collection.

I hope you'll love these characters as much as I have enjoyed writing them.

# VIRGIN

## A SECOND CHANCE ROMANCE

## GEORGIA LE CARRE

GEORGIA LE CARRE

Virgin

You can discover more information about Georgia Le Carre and future
releases here.
https://www.facebook.com/georgia.lecarre
https://twitter.com/georgiaLeCarre
http://www.goodreads.com/GeorgiaLeCarre
978-1-910575-75-8

*Many thanks to:*

*Editors: Caryl Milton, Elizabeth Burns*
*Contributors: IS Creations*
*Cover Art: MG Bookcovers & Designs*
*Proofreader: http:// http://nicolarheadediting.com/*
*French Translation: Gribouille Inconnue*
*Last minute proofing : Brittany Urbaniak & Tracy Gray*

"It's nothing."

"Tyson Friedman, if you don't tell me right now, I swear, I'm going to ground you for a whole week."

I stare into her eyes rebelliously. Let her. I don't care if she does.

"Please, Ty, tell me," she begs. She knows I can never resist her when she pleads for something.

"Johnny Matteson called you a whore, and said I was the son of a gyppo. I punched him and his gang jumped on me."

She blinks in shock then draws a sharp breath. I see her throat work as she swallows hard. Releasing my chin, she straightens. Her eyes flick away from me as she sways unsteadily inside her dressing gown. On TV the music for Countdown starts. It is one of her favorite shows. My mother is clever and often she has the answers before the clock stops ticking. Her hands shake as she flicks a lock of hair from her forehead.

"Mary Mayweather must have started that rumor. I'll go to the school tomorrow and talk to the headmaster," she says vaguely. We both know she'll do no such thing. By tonight she'll be so drunk she'll have forgotten the entire incident.

I touch her arm. "Is it true? Is my father a gyppo?"

She drops to her knees, her eyes suddenly fierce. She still loves him. Desperately. "He's not a ... gyppo. He's a traveler. A wild and beautiful gypsy."

I stare at her face curiously. How transformed it is when she speaks of him. "Where is he now?"

She shakes her head. "It's not important."

"Tell me about my father, Mom. Please." I look at her with begging eyes.

"When you grow up I'll tell you."

I shake my head in frustration. "Why should Mary Mayweather know more about my father than me? If you don't tell me I'll never be able to protect myself against the lies of Johnny Matteson and the other kids."

For a long time she says nothing. Then she nods. "Come," she says, and takes me to her room. It smells in mom's room of stale sweat and alcohol. She sits on the bed and pats the place next to her. I position myself beside her. Taking a deep breath, she opens her drawer and pulls out an old Bible. From between the pages she pulls out a polaroid strip. One of those you get from photo booths. She strokes the length of it lovingly before she hands it to me. "That's your father."

I take it in my hand and stare at the picture. I cannot believe that young laughing girl who looks so full of life and vitality is my mom. She is unrecognizable. I stare at the man, drinking in his features. He has the same coloring as me, straight dark hair and bright blue eyes.

"Does he know about me?"

"He knew I was pregnant."

"Where is he now?" I gasp. My voice is awed. All my life I've wondered about my father. My mother never wanted to speak of him. Every time I asked she would start crying so I stopped asking, even though the questions burned inside me.

She smiles sadly. "He lives in Chertsey."

"Can we go and see him?"

Tears start rolling down her eyes. "No."

I take her hand in mine. Already mine are almost as big as hers. "Don't cry, Mom. Please, don't cry." I hate to see my mother cry, but I have to know about my father. I want my father to come and save us. I want him to make my mother stop drinking. I want her to go back to being the happy girl in the picture. "Does he not want us?"

She shakes her head.

"Why?" I whisper.

"Because …" her voice trembles, "because … he already has another family."

My eyes widen with astonishment. "Another family?" I echo.

"Yes, he has a wife and children," she sobs.

"Children? He has other children."

"Yes." She closes her eyes and tries to compose herself.

"How many?"

"Three boys and a girl."

"I have three half brothers and a half sister."

"Yes," she admits.

"Do they know about me?"

She shakes her head vigorously. "No. No one knows about us. And you must promise never to tell anyone about this."

"What's my father's name?"

"It's not important."

"Tell me. I must know. I have a right, Mom."

"What difference would it make?"

"I want to know. I deserve to know."

She bites her lip.

"Please, Mom. I'll never tell."

She hesitates.

"I promise I'll never tell anyone."

"You must never tell anyone," she cries.

"I'll swear I'll never tell."

"Your father's name is Patrick Eden."

(ONE WEEK LATER)

"What d'ya want with Patrick Eden?" the man growls. His eyes are black and full of suspicion.

I look up at him without flinching. "I'm a friend of his son."

He narrows his eyes. "Which son?"

"Jake. Jake Eden."

"It's the house with the blue curtains." He points a dirty finger down the road.

"Thanks Mister," I say and set off down the road. The house is opposite a field and beyond woods. There are caravans at the end of it. I walk past the house and make for the trees bordering the field. It has been raining. I cross the rain soaked grass and lie down on my stomach in a hollow in the ground. The smell of the wet earth fills my nostrils. The scent of the leaves is fresh and good. This is a good part of the world. Not like Kilburn. Where it smells of traffic and smoke and despair. The grass is cold on my bare legs.

Lying on my belly, I wait.

## (NINE YEARS OLD)

I pour the hot coffee into the flask and press the stopper lip on its mouth then screw on the cap. I put it on the breakfast tray next to the buttered toast, pop out two headache tablets into a small plastic cup, and carry the tray to my mother's bedroom. This is my ritual every day before I go to school. By the time mom wakes up the toast will be cold, but she says she doesn't mind. The most important things are the two headache tablets and the hot coffee.

I open her door and set the tray on her bedside table. The smell in my mother's room is intolerable. Especially now in winter when the windows cannot be opened much and the stench is all pervasive. As a rule I never linger. I turn away, but something catches my attention.

Mom's hand.

Hanging over the edge of the bed. Even in that fleeting glance my brain instinctively notes the stillness, the blue of the fingernails. Slowly, I turn back and look at her face. It is buried in the pillow. I touch her shoulder and jerk back.

Her body is as cold as ice.

Terror grips my body. "Mom," I whisper. My voice is hoarse with fear.

I stare at the still body.

"Mom."

The body doesn't move.

"MOM."

Nothing.

I grasp her shoulders and shake her. Her body is stiff. I turn her around. There is vomit around her mouth and down her chin, neck, clothes. Her eyes are closed. I stare at her dead face for the longest time. Then I put her back on the pillow and go to the living room. I call the police. Calmly, I tell them my mother is dead and give them my address. Then I go back to my mother's room and open the windows. Cold air rushes in.

I cannot have the police smell my mother. I cannot have anyone think less of my mother. I clean off the vomit. I change her nightdress. Her underwear looks yellowed and dirty. I pull it off her thin legs. Her smell is now overpowering. I run some hot water into a basin and squeeze some shower gel into it. Gently, I wash her body with a hand towel. Then I take a fresh set of clothes from the cupboard and dress her in them. I comb her hair and powder her face. I find a case of pink lipstick and carefully drag it over her cold lips. I liberally douse her body with perfume. Lily of the Valley. It stings my nose.

I spray her bedclothes and the entire room with the same bottle.

I don't close the windows, because I've learned that her smell gathers very quickly when the windows are shut. The scent of her perfume is overpowering. There is no way for the other smell to overtake it. The police will be here soon.

She looks quite pretty so I don't cover her face.

I don't feel fear or pain. Comfortably numb, I sit on a chair and wait for the police to arrive. They come with an ambulance. The men pronounce her dead immediately and take her away on a stretcher.

A policewoman sits me down at the kitchen table. She smiles kindly at me. "Where's your father?" she asks.

"I have no father."

She looks concerned. "Do you have grandparents?"

I shake my head

"What about uncles and aunties?"

I shake my head again. My mother was an orphan. She grew up in a foster care system that she hated. She always swore that she would never let the state get their hands on me. When social workers used to come to visit, both my mother and I would pretend that she had stopped drinking.

She frowns. "Do you have no one at all?"

I think of my father holding my half sister high above his head and swinging her around. I think of them laughing. I think of them going into the house with their presents. I think of the promise I made to my mother. I will never betray her. Not as long as I live.

"No," I say quietly.

That slight hesitation makes her frown. "You will have to go to a foster home if you have no one. Are you sure you have absolutely no one?"

"Yes, I'm sure," I say flatly. My voice rings in my head.

# TYSON

## PRESENT DAY

https://www.youtube.com/watch?v=wFhs7WVvuXk
Thunder

"For a fuckin' tight bastard Brad Sommers sure knows how to throw a lavish party," I observe, looking around the luxurious penthouse. It's overflowing with beautiful people he has flown in from all over the world to enjoy his hospitality, admire his generosity, and envy his great fortune. This party is supposed to be in my honor, but in fact he wants the whole world to know he is the proud owner of Magnificent Obsession, the champion horse I bred for him.

"Yeah," Chaz agrees with a laugh. "When he throws a party, you have to look past the fact that he is a total dick. Anyway, you bloody deserve this bash. How do you do it? How can you tell that a three-year old foal will become a champion horse?"

"I don't know. I just do," I say with a shrug. It's true. There is no science to it. It is pure instinct. Horses are my work, my life, and my passion. I have no time for human beings. They are disloyal, greedy, cruel, ungrateful, self-obsessed, vain creatures. Horses. They are gentle beasts capable of great love. Every horse I have bred I have loved with all my heart.

Kinda breaks my heart even now to know Magnificent Obsession will be the property of such a shallow philistine like Brad. He'll never see her as anything more than an expensive bit of horseflesh with the potential to bring him the fame and adulation he craves. I wish she could've gone to someone a little more worthy of her. Somebody who could appreciate her as more than a fast set of hooves.

Chaz throws an arm around my shoulders. "Come on, Tyson. I dare you to show me that all the legends about an Irishman's ability to hold his liquor aren't bullshit."

I chuckle at the challenge. Chaz has no idea. To start with he's been drinking all afternoon, and is already halfway in the bag. Even if he wasn't I could drink him under the table no problem. They didn't call me Hollow Legs back at the young offender's correctional institute in Ashfield for nothing. "You might find yourself regretting that challenge, my friend," I warn.

"Empty words," he taunts with a cheeky smile.

We make our way to one of the three bars set up for just the occasion and I order a double whiskey neat. Chaz wants to see what I can do? Why not?

"There he is!" Brad's enthusiastic voice booms over the party noises from across the room. I wince inwardly as I turn to face him. "The miracle worker! The man who's gonna get me a permanent seat in the winner's circle! You should come work for me. I promise to make it worth your while."

I laugh, but it's strained. I regard him from above the rim of my glass. I received his payment for Magnificent Obsession, so I know how much coin he dropped on her, but even the idea of working for him makes my skin itch. "Let's wait until she wins a few more times before you crown me."

"Look at all that modesty." His eyes glitter with excitement.

To a man like him she will always be just an investment. He will never see beyond her shining perfect form. If she was injured tomorrow he would never suffer other than to regret the investment.

He slings a hand up to my shoulders, and I smell sweet champagne on his breath. "So how do you like it?" he asks, swinging his arm in an arc to encompass the entire suite. It's grand, to be sure, with its high ceilings—four or five meters, in my estimation—and windows which stretch the full height and length of three walls, granting guests an incredible night view of the twinkling lights of Paris. Fuck knows what he paid for the privilege.

"It's like sitting on a cloud, looking down on the city below," I sum up.

Throwing his head back, he starts cackling like a fucking hyena, the action pitches him off-balance and he starts to fall backwards. I catch him in time to keep him from cracking his head open on his fine Italian marble floor. He pats me on the hand as I set him upright.

He winks at me. "Magnificent Obsession is a hell of a lot prettier and faster than any blue-chip share."

If I stay around him any longer my fist is going to end up connecting with his jaw. I take a belt from my whiskey. I look around and wonder where the hell Chaz escaped to.

He leans against the bar and looks at me with a sly expression. "Actually, I could introduce you to a few pretty things that are so fast they'll make you see Jesus!"

Before I can react, he signals to a woman in a long red dress and she immediately starts walking towards us. One look at her and I can see that she is a high-class hooker. I finish my whiskey and signal to the bartender to refresh my drink.

"Helllllllo," she drawls.

"Be nice to him," Brad says, and walks away.

"Gosh, you're a good looking one," she says looking up into my eyes and running her manicured nails along my jacket lapel. Her perfume lingers in the air between us.

"Listen, I'm flying out tonight. So this might not be such a good idea …" I shrug.

"I don't need the whole night," she whispers.

I take her hand in mine and put it on the bar. "Thanks sweetheart, but I'm not really in a party mood tonight."

"That's a pity. We would have had a great time together," she says, and even manages to look regretful.

I leave her and take a slow walk around the perimeter of the room. It seems like some of the most beautiful women in Europe are gathered in Brad's vast living room.

"See anything you like?" Chaz asks from my side.

"How the hell do you randomly pop up out of nowhere?" I

ask with a frown. "And while I'm at it, where the fuck did you disappear to while I was trying to keep myself from punching Brad in the mouth?"

"Oh, sorry about that," he says with a sly grin. "I was busy. A redhead pulled me aside and asked me a thousand questions about you. Beauty she was too ... fucking legs that went up to her neck."

I take a sip of my whiskey. "Really now? Why didn't she come up to me herself?"

He shrugs. "I'm not as intimidating as you. Women see a short guy with a dad bod and automatically think he's easy to talk to. One of the many misconceptions I have to deal with on a daily basis."

"Like they don't warm up real quick when they find out how full your bank accounts are," I say dryly.

"If I can keep them hanging around long enough to find out," he points out, laughing.

I scan the room lazily, my eyes traveling over the many firm, half-naked bodies, some of which sway in time with the music pumping out of Brad's exceptional sound system. More than a few of them notice me sizing them up and flash "come hither" smiles my way. I've learned to not let it go to my head ... too much. I'm only a man, after all. "Which one is she?" I ask.

"There she is." Chaz points across the room to a corner. Four girls sitting on a sofa. Sure enough, one of them is a stunning redhead. Porcelain skin, sapphire eyes, and a body that would tempt the devil himself. Yes, she's very tasty, but it's not her my eyes can't get enough of. It's the girl sitting next to her.

"Who's the girl on her left?" I ask, eyes glued.

"Which one? The blonde?"

"Yeah. The blonde."

"No idea, mate. If you're not going to have the redhead …"

He's still talking, but I stop hearing him. I can't break focus. The blonde is all I can look at, all I can think about. Her hair shines like gold, and she swings it from side to side as she laughs at something one of her friends said. The light shines directly on her and her eyes are emeralds, sparkling and clear. Her full lips curve into a smile as she playfully shoves the redhead.

"**D**on't start," I warn, slapping Kylie's arm.

"What?" she protests, pretending innocence. "I'm just saying that Paris slash this party could be a great place for you to find a man to pop your cherry."

"I'm not here to find a man to … to … pop my cherry, as you so elegantly put it. I'm here to attend Charlotte's wedding tomorrow," I splutter with embarrassment. I can't believe this topic has come up again.

"Far be it for me to agree with Kylie," Lina pipes up, "but she does have a point. We are in the city of love. I mean, look around you. What better place to find a lover than here? I've seen at least three guys that I'd personally love to climb up. Plus, we're in a foreign country. Other than us no one else need ever know. You could let your hair down, be completely slutty, do whatever you want, as long as it's legal, of course, and be back at work on Monday with no one the wiser."

I sigh heavily. How I wish I had never told Charlotte I was still a virgin. She told Lina, Lina told Catherine, Catherine told Kylie, and now every damn person in our circle knows. If I didn't believe in my own convictions so strongly I would be almost tempted to lose my virginity just to stop them gossiping and speculating endlessly about my sex life.

"What are you waiting for, anyway?" Kylie joins in gleefully. "You're already twenty-two. Your poor pussy is going to shrivel up and die if you carry on depriving her of her protein shake. Sex is a healthy thing. Think of it as a sport."

Both Lina and Catherine laugh at the joke. I lean forward and speak earnestly, willing them to understand, even though I know there is not a hope in hell that I will convince them. "For me sex is not a bit of sport. I want my first time to be with the guy of my dreams. I want it to mean something special. I want it to be," I pause, "everything."

"Oh, Izzy, Lina says with a sigh. "You are going to be very disappointed if that is what you imagine losing your virginity is all about. The first time is only great in romance novels. Unless you find a man with a magic penis it's going to be painful, awkward, and messy. There might even be blood."

I frown. I don't want to hear their well-meaning advice. I know it's going to be painful. I know there might be blood. But they are still talking about it from a physical perspective. They don't understand. I'm talking about the deep emotional connection between a man and a woman. Maybe I'm a fool, maybe they are right, such a thing doesn't exist. But I'm not giving up on my dream.

"Once I wanted everything too," Kylie says, flicking her flame colored hair forward. "Now, I'd settle for a man who can give me one night of great mindless sex. Like that horse trainer guy that this party is in honor of, Tyson Eden. Oh my God!

He's so delectable I want to throw my panties at him. His reputation is love 'em and leave 'em, but by God, I would let him fuck me until I couldn't walk straight."

Lina laughs loudly. "I think I just want a man who will take good care of me financially. Some of these men are so wealthy they could set you up for life. Someone like Brad Sommers. He gave his last girl an apartment in Knightsbridge and a sports Mercedes. Even after he broke up with her he still paid for all her credit card bills. He only stopped when she hooked up with that Polo player."

I crinkle my nose. "I'd rather be a spinster for the rest of my life than end up with any of the men in here. They're all way out of my league. Too rich and glamorous for me. I'm not interested in a man who is so wealthy he could have any woman. I mean, why would such a man settle down with one woman? The temptation would be incredible. All I want is an ordinary man that I can have a family with."

"That's very sweet, Izzy," Lina says, "but don't you think you're being a bit naïve? Trust me when I say, without money love will fly out of the window so fast it'll leave you reeling."

"I think you're wrong," I insist stubbornly. "Real love doesn't need money. I'd prefer to live in a cold, cramped apartment with a man I love than in a palace with one I don't. I'm looking for my soulmate."

"Oh, don't be such a goose. There is no such thing as a soulmate. Show me a relationship that lasts and I'll show you a woman who is making all kinds of sacrifices and compromises to make it work. You're crazy if you think you'll find a man like that. Any man, rich or poor, would cheat given half the chance. If I could have a man like Brad Sommers I'd be set for life. Who cares about hearts and flowers? I'll settle for throbbing chemistry, diamonds and Guccis."

I put my cocktail glass down. "Okay, you girls have fun. I have to get back to the hotel. I promised Charlotte that I'd go out early and get replacement ribbons for her."

"Don't be such a party pooper." Kylie groans. "Things have not even begun to warm up yet and you're already wanting to leave. Do you know how many arms I had to twist to get us on the guest list?"

"Bullshit," calls Lina. "You flirted with one of the bouncers and he sneaked us in."

"I don't see you getting us into any happening parties," Kylie snaps back.

"Look, I'm really sorry. I don't want to ruin the night for anybody," I apologize to everyone at the table. "You guys know this is not my kind of scene. I'm a simple person. I like babies and dogs and I'm happiest when I'm at home in my PJs with a good book and a box of chocolates."

Catherine shakes her head despairingly. "You're going to waste your life away, babe. One day you'll look in the mirror and think where the fuck did my youth go, but it will be too late then."

"Oh my God, yes! Tall, dark and hunky alert at four o'clock," Lina mouths, her eyes enormous. "Look, but not all at once, please. Since you're the virgin you may look first, Izzy."

"For God's sake it's not a disease, you know," I mutter, trying not to grit my teeth with irritation.

"I'll look," Lina offers brightly. She toys with her earring before turning her head casually. Very calmly she swivels around and looks at me with widened eyes. "Jesus H Christ. There is a hot devil wearing black jeans and ... he's staring right at you, Izzy."

"Whoa ... and he hasn't even seen your big, heart-shaped butt yet," Catherine quips.

"Don't be so silly," I grumble, feeling myself flush with embarrassment. It's obvious that if he has both Lina and Catherine open-mouthed with wonder then he is definitely not staring at me when the whole place is crawling with beauties and models.

"See for yourself if you don't believe me, but take six deep breaths first," she says.

Something about her widened eyes makes my stomach contract nervously.

"Hang on. Hang on," Kylie cuts in suddenly. "That guy is mine. That's Tyson Eden, the horse guy that I was telling you about. I saw him first so you all can just lay off him, okay?"

But nothing can stop my head from turning. From looking at the devil himself.

# TYSON

**"Lovers don't finally meet somewhere,
they are in each other all along."
- Rumi**

When she turns her head and looks at me, she might as well have punched me in the gut. Our eyes lock and all the air escapes my lungs. Desire, hot and urgent, claws in my gut. I want to do things to her I have never done to any other woman. At that moment the craving is so strong I could have climbed any mountain, swam any ocean to have her. If I don't end up between her creamy legs tonight, my name is not Tyson.

"Earth to Tyson," Chaz laughs. "Wow. She sure did something to you, pal. Do you need a ride to the jewelers to pick up a ring?"

"Stuff it," I growl. He's still laughing as I head for her table. No way I'm letting her out of my sight. I need to know her. I need to do more, far more, than know her. My blood throbs in my veins and my cock shoves against the zipper of my jeans.

The chicks stop laughing as I approach. One of them looks away. They were definitely talking about me. The redhead who wanted me pushes her chest out.

"Good evening, ladies," I say with a slow grin.

The other women are all staring at me, but I don't even see them. I zero in on the blonde. Her eyes are trained on me. They are bright, bright green. The brightest I've seen. Bedroom eyes.

"Enjoying the party?" I drawl, not taking my eyes off her. She's really something. The dress she's wearing comes down to her knees, and any man knows that's even sexier than a woman who puts everything out on display.

She flicks the tip of her pink tongue over her lips in a nervous gesture, and my eyes drop down to her mouth. Oh, Fuck! That mouth. An image of my cock in it flashes into my head. I can already see her long, sun-kissed legs open and waiting. Hell, I can't remember the last time a woman had such an effect on me. I stare at her in bemused fascination.

"It's … nice. Are you enjoying it?" Her voice flows over my heated skin like warm honey. Hell, I could listen to her read a dictionary … in my bed.

I lean in. "I wasn't … until just now."

The other two girls titter, probably surprised by my direct technique, but the redhead is not giving up. "You're the man of the hour, aren't you? Seems a shame you weren't enjoying a party held in your honor," she purrs.

I drag my eyes away from the blonde to the redhead. She crosses her legs. There's a lot of her on show. She looks me up and down, one eyebrow arched. That look pretty much always guarantees a good night, but it leaves me cold. No, it's the blonde with the butter-wouldn't-melt-in-her-mouth expression, the modest skirt, and the two little dimples in her cheeks that I'm hot for.

I turn my focus back to my quarry. "You girls seem to know a lot about me. I feel at a disadvantage," I murmur.

"Unlike you, we're not famous. And we don't make it a point to get our pictures in all the juiciest gossip rags, either," the redhead says.

A slow smile spreads over my face as I stare at the blonde. She stares back, as helpless to look away as I am. "Yeah, well, I don't make it a point. It just turns out that way. I guess they think I'm photogenic."

My blonde bites her plump bottom lip to stop herself from smiling. "I guess they must do."

For a few seconds, it might as well have been just the two of us at the table—hell, in the entire suite. One of the other girls clears her throat a little too loudly before she gets up and pulls the redhead to her feet. "Right, we'll be on the dance-floor if you need us,' she says.

"Okay," Blondie says not breaking eye contact with me.

I barely look at them as I slide into a chair next to her. She smells as good as she looks.

"I could keep playing word games with you, but it's all a waste of time." I hold out my hand. "My name is Tyson. But you already knew that, right?"

She nods, placing her hand in mine. It's small, delicate, the skin silky soft. "Izzy."

"Izzy?" Fitting name for that odd mix of innocence and unconscious sex appeal.

She nods, and as I watch, her cheeks start filling with color. I don't think it's the cocktails doing that, just like my whiskey isn't making my cock throb. Who'd have thought? All from holding a girl's hand. Yup, she's blushing because I'm still holding on to her hand, long after any ordinary handshake should have come to an end. I want to touch more than just her hand. I want to slide my hand up her skirt and hear her scream when I suck her clit into my mouth.

She withdraws first, sliding her smooth skin over mine, and taking possession of her glass once again. "So, you train horses?"

"I breed them," I correct quietly.

"Oh." The corners of her mouth curve down. She is not pretty. There's nothing pretty about her. She is a river of sexy. "What's the difference?"

"It's pretty simple. I maintain my horses, make sure they get the right care and exercise, eat as they should, and when the time comes, I pay for the stud with the best qualities and … well, you know …" I finish with a wink.

She flushes again, stronger this time. "You play a little romantic music, dim the lights, and let nature take its course?"

I have to laugh. "Eh, maybe not exactly like that, but you get the general idea. We have an exceptional stable of champion horses—including a few former champions who are now out to stud. Maggie's father was a champion."

"Maggie?"

It's my turn to flush a little. Nobody knows of my little nickname but me. "Magnificent Obsession. It's just easier to call her Maggie. Rolls off the tongue."

"I can tell you care about her," she observes with a soft smile.

"You can now?"

She nods firmly, convinced, sincere ... breathtakingly beautiful. "Sure. Your eyes lit up when you mentioned her."

I can't help but shift uncomfortably when she reveals me like that. It's rare for me to even have a conversation about anything deeper than what a woman wants to drink or whether she needs me to call her a taxi in the morning. The way she looks at me, though. The way her own eyes light up.

"Yes, I guess I do care about her," I admit with a shrug. "She's a special horse. I was there when her mother foaled and I've been raising her since the first day. She's damned fast, too. I only hope Brad knows what he's doing and gets the right people working with her."

Izzy's hand covers mine. Jesus! Goosebumps. "You're very sweet."

My eyes widen. Sweet? Not exactly something I'm used to hearing from a woman. "Yeah, well, I have my moments. What about you? What do you do?"

"Oh, nothing as exciting as you," she says, waving the hand that's no longer touching me. "I'm no big deal. Someone's unappreciated assistant."

"What do you want to be one day?"

She frowns again. Deeper this time. "Why do I have to want to be anything else?"

Ouch. "I didn't say you had to. But normally, a person doesn't want to stick with a job they feel so ..."

"So blah about?"

I chuckle. "Yes. So blah about. You should do something that excites you, something that makes you want to get out of bed every morning. Does your job do that for you?" I lean in a little closer and get another whiff of her perfume, and something else. Shampoo? Soap? Her natural smell? It's enough to make me want to bury my nose in the crook of her neck and never come up for air.

"Obviously not," she giggles.

"What are you enthusiastic about?" I ask, looking her straight in the eye.

A secret smile plays over her lips. "I don't know, truth be told. I don't know if I have anything that I'm all that enthusiastic about."

"You're probably too young." I grin. I know she has a dream. She just doesn't want to share it with me. I'll work it out of her. I want all her secrets.

"I'm twenty-two."

I wave a dismissive hand. "A mere child."

"Oh, what are you? Five minutes older?" She laughs.

I decide to take a chance. "My point is, you have plenty of

time to find out what excites you." My hand finds her knee and rests there gently.

One corner of her luscious mouth quirks up in a knowing smile. "Oh, I already know that. No problems there." She doesn't move my hand away.

"Really now? You'll have to tell me all about it."

"It's not the sort of thing I like to discuss in public." She glances around the room. "I mean, so many strangers. So much bad dancing."

I chuckle and let my eyes stray around the room. She's not wrong about that. Everybody's a little worse for drink by now. A bunch of moose in high heels got loose could be a good way to describe what is happening in the center of the room. Brad's probably in the center of it all, living it up. "Maybe we should get out of here so you can tell me more," I suggest.

She bites down on that juicy bottom lip. Something I plan on doing myself later tonight. "Are you hungry?"

She shrugs. "I suppose I could eat."

"Good. My hotel has a fantastic room service menu."

She bursts out laughing, and that's the sexiest thing of all.

"What?" I ask.

"You're direct as hell."

I blink. Is she really that oldest of clichés—a good girl? Do they even exist anymore? Not in my experience. "Too forward, huh?"

"No, I just expected you to be a lot smoother."

I grin. "Baby, I can be smoother. Some parts of me are so smooth you'll have to touch to believe."

"I can't believe you said that," she blurts out, her cheeks flaring up with heat.

I take pity on her. "Want to see Paris by night?"

That goes down well, her eyes sparkle. "Really?"

I shrug. "Sure. You ready to go?"

"You want us to leave now?" she asks incredulously.

"Why not?"

"But the party's for you!"

"Yeah, well, between you and me and the designer walls, I think it's more a party for the man throwing it than it is for me. But as I say …" I hold a finger to my lips.

She smiles. "But I don't know you at all. You could be a secret serial killer."

I look into her eyes and words I have never said to anyone pour out of my mouth. "You know me, Izzy. You've always known me."

She stares into my eyes, her smile dying away. "You're right. I do know you." She says something else, but I don't quite catch it. It sounds like: I've been waiting for you all my life. But obviously, that can't be what she said.

I hold out my hand and she places hers into it. I watch her stand in a single graceful movement. She's only average height, coming up to my shoulder in a pair of heels, but her body makes my mouth water. Her black dress leaves a lot to the imagination, but it can't hide her delicious curves.

"Where will we go?"

"Do you like dancing?"

She nods, a smile playing about her lips.

"Do you like drinking Jameson?"

The smile becomes a grin. "I'm not adverse to trying it."

I pull her close to my body. "Want to go to a sixties club called Le Coq?"

She nods. "I should tell my friends first, though."

I turn my head. "No need. Just wave to them. I think they get the picture."

She blushes deep red as she waves goodbye to the three girls gawking at us.

# IZZY

https://www.youtube.com/watch?v=d8VbeXzdWWM
Nightcall

I've left a party on the arm of a stranger. Not just any stranger, either, but one the gossip magazines claim is an infamous cad, the type to love 'em and leave 'em.

I don't do things like this!

I've never left a party with a strange man, no matter how sexy he was, or how blue his eyes were, or how thick and rich his hair was. Just because I want to tangle my fingers in Tyson's black mane and never let go, or that his smile makes my toes curl, I shouldn't be leaving with him.

But I am.

I used to shake my head condescendingly when I read about girls who got suckered in by a sexy smile, or a great pair of eyes.

Now I get it.

It's not just the smile or the eyes, though they count too. It's the way someone makes you feel when they look at you. When we were at that party, surrounded by a hundred other people, he made me feel as if I was the only woman in the room, no, make that in the world. Nobody else existed. Not even Kylie, and she's the one men normally trip over me to get closer to. Not that I do badly on my own, but when I'm with her I might as well switch off the lights and go to bed: I'm invisible.

Except with him.

He is so tall I have to throw my head back to look at him. Not conventionally good-looking, but dark and hawkish. Almost dangerous and irresistibly seductive. And the hunger in his eyes! That is a damn beautiful thing. My heart is beating wildly in my ribcage, as we go down the thickly carpeted corridor and step into the lift. The doors swish close. In the electric atmosphere we don't talk. I watch our reflections in the highly polished doors.

Tyson is leaning against the back wall, hands shoved into the pockets of his jeans. I can't stop looking at the black shirt he's wearing, the way the top buttons are undone, showing off a delectable triangle of chiseled golden chest. I lift my eyes to his and our gazes meet. The naked lust in his eyes makes me tingle from head to toe.

"Are you a friend of Brad's?" he asks.

"Oh, no, Kylie got us all into the party. She's the one with the red hair," I explain. I wish my pulse would stop fluttering so frantically.

"Ah, I see. I should have introduced myself to everyone before moving in on you. I suppose you'll get an earful tomorrow."

"That's a very unlikely scenario. They'll want an earful from me—didn't you notice them all staring at us with their mouths and eyes open wide as we left?"

He grins. "No, it's something that can't be unseen."

I laugh even though I am still shocked by my own bold behavior.

"Are you girls on holiday?"

"No, we're here for my friend's wedding. It's tomorrow and we're all bridesmaids."

"Ah."

The lift opens out to the lobby. He holds my elbow. It's not a firm grip, but the sort of thing that clearly lets people know I'm with him. It's sexy in a possessive, caveman way. I like it. The night porter nods at us as we pass him by. Outside, the night is hot and dark. The way it has never felt to me before. I take a deep breath to clear my head. I feel almost giddy with the thrill of his presence.

"Where are we headed?" I ask as he hails a taxi.

He looks at his watch. "We're going to a club, but we're also just in time to see the Eiffel Tower."

I smile. "I've seen it."

"Ah, but you haven't seen what it does every hour on the hour from ten to midnight, have you?"

I shake my head. My expression is curious, but he doesn't explain.

He puts me into the taxi and goes over to the other side.

He tells the driver the name of the street, but I don't catch it. "Take the route that passes the Eiffel Tower," he instructs.

The driver who has a shock of curly dark hair nods. "*Oui.*"

Sitting so close without all the other aromas of the bar, I smell him. He smells like a man should. Woodsy with the faint smell of leather and spice. I look up at him. Even in the dark his eyes are too bright. Too blue. Like slicked topaz jewels. My mouth parts.

"I want a taste," he says, his voice guttural.

Without waiting for a reply, his hands tighten around my upper-arms and his face descends. He stops half-an-inch away from me and inhales deeply as if he is breathing in my essence. Gently he licks my lips. Desire sears my insides, making my thighs clench.

"Peach?"

"Peach schnapps cocktail," I gasp unsteadily.

Then, his lips capture my mouth, and he takes.

And takes.

And takes.

As if he has been starving for me. The hunger makes my head spin. My body arches towards him, my hands desperately clawing his shirt, pulling him closer.

The taxi driver coughs loudly.

I pull away, flushed, embarrassed, and amazed by my behavior. Unable to tear my eyes away from his heavy-lidded ones I stare disbelievingly into them.

"The lights, Izzy," Tyson whispers, huskily.

I turn my head then, and for a second, my dazed brain computes what I see as an effect of the kiss, a hallucination. Because the tower seems to be sparkling, the lights twinkling, and flashing really fast. I blink a few times in astonishment before I realize that it must be the special effect that Tyson wanted to show me. The road turns off and we start driving parallel to it. I turn back to watch it. When I swivel my head back to Tyson, he is watching me.

"Thank you for showing me. It's beautiful," I murmur.

"My pleasure," he says, and the way he looks at me makes my throat close over.

He doesn't touch me again, but sitting next to him, my whole body tingles with excitement as we drive through the streets of Paris. He seems happy enough just to be going somewhere with me, which warms me up inside.

I turn my head and stare at the scenery, but once our eyes meet, I forget to breathe. How is it possible that I feel like I know him when we only just met? When I look at him and he looks at me, I can almost hear his thoughts. I bet we could have a whole conversation without saying a word.

When the taxi stops, he hands the driver some money. Grabbing my hand, he yanks me out of the seat with him. I land on my feet and, filled with awe at the adventure my life has become, look up into his face.

The wind catches his hair, plays with it, and throws it across his forehead. He pushes it away as it starts to rain. A fine mist that soaks my upturned face.

"Come on," he says. Holding me close, he takes me through a set of wooden doors.

Le Coq is heaving. He clears a path for me through the solid wall of people. I notice them looking at him, parting to make way for him. He is so big and commanding. We go past a zinc bar and reach another door with a doorman.

He nods at Tyson and beckons us through. We go down some stone steps, and open another door.

It is like going back in time.

# IZZY

https://www.youtube.com/watch?v=TqL_pinZVp8
Tutti Frutti

"Oh," I exclaim, "it's like we are in a dance hall in sixties America." Waitresses dressed in sixties mini-dresses and beehive wigs pass by balancing trays of drinks. There is a little stage where a rock and roll band is performing, people are dancing to their lively music, and the atmosphere is amazing.

"Like it?" Tyson shouts over the fantastic din.

"I love it," I scream.

Tyson spots a small table in the corner where we can hole up and pulls me along. A waitress arrives almost immediately.

"Jameson?" he mouths to me.

I nod.

He shows her two fingers and she takes his credit card and puts a pink marker on the table to indicate that we are her customers before sashaying away. My head and body move in time to the quick and catchy beat of the music. I look at the dancers twisting on the dancefloor and their energy is astonishing. Some of them are really good. The men pick up women, swing them over their heads and catch them again. *Tutti Frutti* comes on.

"Wanna dance?" Tyson shouts.

"I can't do these sixties moves," I protest, horrified.

"I'll show you," he says and stands. Before I can protest he hauls me up, and with his strong hands around my waist propels me towards the dancefloor.

"I can't dance, Tyson," I say, leaning away from him. The last thing I want to do is make a fool of myself when everybody else is so damn good.

He doesn't take no for an answer. He curls his large muscular hand around my waist, and teaches me right there on the dancefloor. His large hands placed somewhere on my body, make it easy for me to follow his lead. He tells me I'm a natural. To my delight, soon I am doing the mash potato, the swim, the twist, and the pony.

"Want to try a lindy hop?" he asks

I laugh, breathless, and happier than I've ever been. "What is that?"

He points to a couple who are doing a fast swing. I watch the woman slide between his legs and get swung up over his head, before she rolls across his shoulder and lands on her feet like a cat.

I shake my head vigorously. "Oh no, no, noooo, Tyson," I scream, as he swings my hand and twirls me around so my back is facing his front. He fits his hands around my waist, hoists me high into the air, and flings me backwards. Earlier, I saw another couple do the same move so I do what the girl thrown into the air did. I bring my knees up so that I somersault in the air and land on my feet. Even before my feet can touch the ground Tyson has turned around and caught both my hands to steady me. I look into his eyes and laugh. I was petrified while I was flying in the air, but suddenly I feel free and filled with energy. I had executed the move successfully and I was never in any danger. Anybody who looked could have seen me flash my underwear, but I don't care. I throw myself into Tyson's arms. He twirls me around and we carry on dancing.

We make a beautiful team.

By the time we return to our table, we are both flushed and hot. Tyson's hair is disheveled and his eyes glitter with something unnameable. He knocks back his Jameson and I follow suit. The alcohol burning all the way down to my stomach. I wipe my mouth. "That was great. How come you're so good with this kind of dancing?"

"It was a pilot program at the boys' correction facility I was in. They wanted to know if teaching little shits dancing would make them less pig-headed."

"Did it?"

He chuckles. "Nope."

I laugh. "Why were you in such a place?"

"I stole a Mitsubishi 4 by 4, took it for a joyride, and caused

43

hundreds of thousands worth of damage when I mowed it into a Lamborghini official dealership."

I clap my hand to my mouth. "Ouch, that was unlucky."

"It wasn't unlucky. I crashed it there deliberately. I was an angry kid. I wanted to destroy precious things. Things I could never hope to have."

"Oh."

"Yup, I hated the world."

"How old were you then?"

He orders two more glasses of Jameson, by lifting his hand and showing the peace sign to the waitress. "Thirteen."

"You were just a child."

He shrugs. "I have a very thick skull."

"Were you in that school for long?"

"I ran away to Ireland when I was fourteen. I would have ended up a criminal, but I stayed a night on someone's farm and he had horses. The moment I touched a horse I knew what I wanted to do for the rest of my life. Until then the world did not make sense."

"Where do you raise your horses?" I ask.

"In Suffolk."

"Ah, I thought your farms were based out of Ireland." He still has a brogue and all.

He shakes his head. "Nah, I left Ireland when I was 20."

"So now you breed horses and sell them to men like Brad?"

He rubs a hand over the back of his neck. "Yeah."

"What's the matter?"

The waitress places two glasses on the table. "You say you're not a friend of Brad's?"

"No. I never heard of him before tonight."

He holds his glass in a mock salute. "Well, since you don't know him, I'll tell you: I wish Maggie went to just about anybody but him. He cares nothing about her. All he wants is the glory she'll bring him."

He looks sad and my heart goes out to him. I never expected him to be such a deep thinker. Kylie had given us the impression he would be loud and brash; desperate for cheap publicity. My hand closes over his before I can think about it. "I'm sorry you have misgivings."

He glances down and smiles just a little, then turns his hand a bit so it locks with mine. "Thanks for listening. It's been weighing on me ever since the sale went through."

"Why sell her to him at all?"

"I made a mistake. I doubled her price because it never crossed my mind that anybody would pay that much," he says, sounding glum. "I wanted to tell him to take a leap, but I couldn't go back on my word."

"The money doesn't matter to you, then?" I ask, a little hopeful.

He grins wryly. "I wouldn't go that far. Money's a wonderful thing to have—the more, the better, but there are things that matter more."

"Noble of you," I say with a smirk.

He raises an eyebrow. "What's that mean?"

"It means it's very easy for a person with all the money in the world to be choosy. Some of us have to do what we have to do. Don't get me wrong, I think it's wonderful that you care about your horse, I really do. You're not half as shallow as the gossip mags make you out to be."

"Thanks, I think."

"It was meant as a compliment." I finish off my drink, then tell myself I absolutely should not have another one if I want to keep control of myself. "As I was saying, though, it's nice that you even have a choice whether you should or shouldn't take the money."

"Is that why you work at a job you don't like?"

"I guess I had that coming to me."

"I guess you did. You did just call me shallow."

"Not fair. I said you're not as shallow as the general perception seems to be."

"Oh, right. I got mixed up." He grins.

"To answer your question, yes. It's why I work at a job I don't like. Most people do, don't they? They have to work to make money to support themselves, and it doesn't matter a damn whether or not they like what they do."

He shakes his head, and he's not grinning anymore. "Then the job you are doing is not good enough for you, Izzy. You are so young. The whole world is at your feet."

"Oh, well. Let's not spoil tonight talking about that. Tell

me more about you," I say, sweeping my hair over one shoulder as I silently scream at myself to stop pouring out my stupid heart to him. It's supposed to be a fun night and look at me. He's going to think I'm a complete idiot—a corporate drone, selling her soul in exchange for the monthly rent, babbling on about unimportant nonsense.

"You're the only woman in that entire penthouse I wanted to meet." Those impossibly blue eyes of his make a slow tour of my face. I should want to turn my head away or hold my hands in front of me or something, anything to get him to stop looking. But I don't want him to. I like that he seems to enjoy what he sees.

"I am?" I ask with a breathless giggle.

"Yes. You know that, so don't play coy." He moves closer to me, leaning in as though he wants to speak into my ear. His breath is hot on my neck, the side of my face. So why do goosebumps cover my skin? "The moment I laid eyes on you, I had to know you. I couldn't help myself."

There's no way he's saying these things. I have to be imagining it. He's the infamous Tyson Eden. He could have any woman he wants. I feel the curious looks from other girls around. I have been feeling them all night, ever since he came to sit with me.

But he wants me. Me!

I down the amber liquid in my glass and feel it hit my empty stomach. The alcohol is like fire in my veins, making me brazen. "I don't particularly want to spend all night here," I whisper, getting as close as I dare to his ear. The scent of his cologne is enough to force a groan from deep in the back of my throat. I've never had such a primal reaction to a man in my life.

He leans back just enough to look in my eyes, and when he does I'm finished. I'm his.

"Really," he drawls, one eyebrow shooting up. God, he has such a sexy smile.

"Really." I rest my hand on his shoulder. A very firm, very broad shoulder. I can feel his muscles flexing under the perfectly tailored suit jacket and realize with a thrill that shoots straight between my legs that he'll be stripping that jacket off soon enough.

I can't wait.

# IZZY

"It was like one solid wall of humanity in there!" I say, laughing and shaking out the wrinkles in my dress when we manage to fight our way outside. The air has cooled somewhat and the night seems mysterious and full of wonder. I look up into his eyes and stop laughing, caught by the hunger blazing in them. He really wants me. One day, I will tell my grandchildren; the most unexpected, most unimaginable, most awesome thing happened to me when I went to Paris to be my best friend's bridesmaid.

He slides one hand along the back of my head and pulls me towards him. I feel his fingers running through my hair and the pressure of his palm. The warmth of him envelopes me as I get closer. I feel his breath on my face, and I hear the thudding of my blood in my ears as he dips his head towards me. Our mouths meet, the mellow taste of whiskey on his tongue mingles with mine, and it's pure magic.

My knees turn to jelly and I feel as if I might collapse at his feet. He must have understood this because his other arm encircles my waist firmly as his mouth moves over mine. I'm his. All his. My body melts into him and for that perfect, breathless time, all the pieces fall into place. I am where I belong. I didn't miss anything by not partaking in all the anonymous, frantic, drunken sex that Kylie crows about. I wasn't wrong to wait. They laughed at me, but I wasn't 'being silly' or 'being foolish'. My body always knew this existed. This is what I was waiting for all this time.

By the time the kiss ends, the thick bulge in his jeans is digging into my flesh, and there's an ache between my legs. For the first time in my life I'm hungry for a man to be inside me. Suddenly, it seems urgent that we get to his hotel. Fast. I barely pay attention to the taxi ride. My hands run over his shoulders and arms as he kisses me until I can't even think straight. I actually need his help getting out of the car.

We cross the lobby in large strides. Both of us barely able to keep our hands off each other.

He opens his room door and I almost fall in. Any other time, I would be fascinated by the size and luxury of his suite. I would have spent some time running my hands over the furniture and admiring the view. Instead, I turn around and launch myself into his arms as he kicks the door closed. He lifts me off my feet. I lose my heels on the way to the bedroom. I'm kissing him madly, groping at him like a horny schoolgirl because that's how he makes me feel. It is so wild and crazy it is like something out of a dream.

He sets me down by the edge of the bed and my hands slide under his jacket. I relish the feeling of his powerful shoulders as my hands move over them, pushing the jacket over his arms and letting it drop to the floor. Then my hands lock around his neck as he pulls me in for a deeper kiss. When he grabs my butt in his strong hands and slams my body towards him, I cry out with a strange animal sound.

"You're so fucking delicious," he growls, burying his face in my neck.

I tilt my head back with a sigh, absorbing his touch and the uncontrollable madness of it all. All I want to do is give myself to him, and let him do what he likes because I know I'll like it, too. No man has touched me the way he does. Their lips never started a fire under my skin the way his does. I didn't cry out like an animal when any of them dared to slide a hand under my dress or cup my butt. My nerves are dancing, sending waves of pleasure throughout my body.

I hear my zipper slide down. My dress falls open. His calloused hands on my bare skin is heaven. I wiggle out of the dress, leaving me in nothing but my matching black-lace bra and panties with the pretty pink bow at the front—thank God I didn't just throw on any old thing tonight. He pulls back and looks at me from the top of my head to my painted toes, drinking me in with his eyes. His hands work the buttons on his shirt, but his eyes never leave my body. His nostrils flare as he breathes hard.

The shirt drops and I see that his whole upper-body is inked. Gorgeous animals, angels, skulls, patterns, and crosses run rampant on his big body telling a story of hidden depths. Depths I want to dive into. At that moment I know without any doubt that one day I will get to the bottom of this man.

"So beautiful. God, you're so fucking beautiful," he mutters, taking me in his arms and lowering me to the bed.

I run my hands over his broad back, loving the feel of his silky skin and the corded strength beneath, while he practically … devours me. His tongue reveals my body to me, swirling and licking a trail over my bare skin. Making me feel things I've never felt before. With a deft flick of his fingers, he unclasps my bra and moves the cups aside. His eyes widen when he takes in my full breasts. Then he is hungrily lowering his head. Even before he reaches my skin, my nipples begin to tingle with fierce anticipation.

My back arches and I cry out his name when his warm wet mouth closes over my nipple. My fingers tangle in his thick black hair and I slide one leg up over his. He catches it. Stroking my thigh, his fingers trail further up. It's sensory overload. I can't take it, but I don't want him to ever stop, either.

"Open for me, baby. I want to get my mouth on your sweet pussy."

I part my thighs willingly, and he brushes against my pussy as he moves south. He's still wearing his pants and I'm still wearing my panties, but when the heat of his hardness presses itself against my open pussy, I gasp with shock. The sensation promises so much. He stops and pushes forward with his hips so his cock rubs against me. Heat races through me.

It's so delicious I whimper for more.

So he gives it to me, again and again, until we're humping and grunting and breathless, driving each other crazy, pushing ourselves to the edge. He covers my mouth with his and thrusts his tongue inside, keeping time with the thrusts against my pussy, and I can hardly control myself anymore. It's all too good, too hot, too much. I realize with a mixture of shock and astonishment that I'm about to climax. What will he think of me? Probably the truth. That I'm an inexperienced, absurd thing who gets off just from dry humping.

I pull away from him, clawing at his shoulders, trying to stop myself, but it is already too late. My body tenses as the first wave hits.

"Oh … oh, God …!" I cry as unspeakable pleasure floods every inch of me. When I dare open my eyes, horribly embarrassed that I came so pathetically quickly, I find him smiling down at me with a proud, satisfied look on his face.

"You're amazing," he murmurs before kissing me again.

And again.

Deeper and deeper.

He's hot and ready for me, probably aching the way I was before my release hit. My body responds to the need in him and to my surprise I feel myself yearning for more. I tug at his belt to show him what I want, and that's all it takes.

He breaks the kiss and kneels in front of me, working at his belt, unzipping and dropping his trousers in a blur. I reach for him, caressing his erection through his underwear—it's so big, so thick. When he rips away the material he springs free, veiny and pulsing with need, I wrap my fingers around him eagerly.

"Careful," he chuckles, moving my hand away. But he's not really laughing. His jaw is clenched tight, like he's barely holding onto control as he unrolls a condom. Then, he hooks his fingers under the waistband of my panties—I lift my legs straight up and he drags the lacy scrap down and tosses them aside. When he stretches out on top of me, I welcome him by wrapping my arms around him. Holding him as close as I can, I whisper, "You know the way my friends were staring at us?"

He looks at me distractedly, as if the words are not really hitting home.

"It's because I've never gone home with any man before."

His eyes widen. "Whoa! Back up. What are you trying to tell me?"

I feel my cheeks grow hot. "I've … never been with a man."

"You're a virgin?" he utters incredulously.

I nod slowly.

"Okay," he says slowly, then a thought occurs to him and he frowns and looks at me suspiciously. "You *are* above eighteen, right?"

"I didn't lie before. I am twenty-two."

He exhales with relief. "Phew, for a moment there …"

I bite my lip. "Sorry, I should have told you earlier."

# TYSON

I lay my fingers on her soft lips, "Don't. Don't ever apologize for being untouched."

She stares up at me, her eyes enormous.

Looking into them makes me feel like a lion. I try to wrap my head around the fantastic fact that no other man has had her. Then suddenly: greed. Fuck, I can claim her for me. The sensation the thought produces shocks me. The idea of marking her with my cock is primal, feral, animal-like, and ridiculous, and yet a wild joy erupts in my chest. I bend my head and brush my lips against her forehead, her temple, her nose, her cheek. She's so soft and so delicate. I inhale her scent. I lick her skin. It's like I can't stop touching her. I swoop down and catch her nipple between my teeth. It feels like silk in my mouth. I suck and I bite. She doesn't stop me. She belongs to me. I can do whatever I like.

I push her legs apart and look at what is mine.

Her pink opening looks small and innocent as it drips out sweet nectar for me. A rush of possessive heat fills my gut.

This is all for me and only me. I look over every inch of her. No other man shall touch this.

"Fuck, you look so hot when you are spread open. I want you always like this. Open for me. Every fucking day for the rest of your life."

She flushes with a mixture of sexual excitement and embarrassment and it's just adorable.

I let my hand brush her swollen clit and she gasps. She's so goddamn responsive it blows my mind. The only other time I've dry humped a woman to climax was with the cleaner at the correction center. I was thirteen and she was my first. We did it in the broom cupboard. She smelt of bleach and body odor, but I came in my pants. Since then, I have made many women cum in my lifetime, but this time, with this woman everything is completely different.

"You're my dirty girl, aren't you?"

She bites her bottom lip and nods, and I fucking ache to sink into that wet slit. It's killing me to wait to feel her innocent little cunt wrap around my cock, but I hold back. I'm going to take my time. I'm going to eat her sweet pussy until she sees heaven. I rub her clit in circles and her hips rise off the bed impatiently. I feel it building in both our bodies, the urge to fuck until we are without skin; one animal.

She moans with pleasure when I push a thick finger into her opening. She's so goddamn tight, I'll have to break her in slowly. My cock needs to be able to fit in there. I plunge my thumb into her pussy and watch her eyes widen. Her pussy walls pulse and contract around my thumb. I thrust it in and out and she starts to writhe with pleasure. I use my two fingers on either side of her clit and begin a sawing motion. Her legs start to tense up.

"You like that, baby?" I ask.

"Yes," she groans as she starts riding my hand.

"You want my cock in you?" In fact, my cock wants to go in bare, and my balls hurt to empty my seed in her.

"Yes," she screams as she comes. I watch her face clench, her body arch like a bow, her thighs quiver, her mouth open in amazement as she goes over.

I wait for her to come back. She opens her eyes. Her skin is flushed and glowing. I push two fingers into her while she is relaxed and not expecting it. I bring my fingers coated with her sticky honey and slip it into my mouth. Just as I guessed, she tastes like heaven.

"Oh," she exclaims, surprised.

I dip my fingers into her tight channel again then hold them in front of her mouth. "Taste yourself."

She opens her mouth and, extending a pink tongue, licks my fingers clean. Just like a little cat. My cock twitches at the sight. I slip my fingers into her mouth and she sucks them. I can climax just looking at that.

I suck on her pussy lips, one fat one at a time, luxuriating in the silky feel and taste of them in my mouth. Then, I move down to her slit and lap hungrily at the juices pouring down for a few minutes.

Her hips are rocking desperately, pleading for release so I plunge a finger into her pussy and return my mouth to her clit, and suck on it once more. It hardens in my mouth even as the muscles in her pussy grow tight around my fingers. I know she isn't far from coming, but when she does, it is even more intense than the two before.

Her virgin cunt clenches my fingers tightly, gripping me like a vice, and her eyes flutter shut as her orgasm hits her. This one is a full-body reaction, and I feel a little proud to have drawn it out of her.

Fisting my cock in my hand, I press the tip to her wet opening, and slide against her in a teasing motion. Instead of pushing into her heat, I slide away.

"What's the matter? Don't you want to?" she whispers, her eyes glazed.

"Don't worry, I'm going to fuck you all right, I just don't want to tear you."

I push into her tightness. She lets out a mewling sound and for a few seconds her muscles fight back, but she's so fucking wet my cock tunnels through, and my thickness fills her little cunt. Her mouth opens in a soundless cry.

"It's okay. It'll only hurt for a moment," I say, going completely still to allow her to adjust to my size. She is so tight it feels as if my dick is being squeezed hard. Slowly, I pull out of her and I see the tinge of red slick on my dick. Jesus, I drew blood. How strange that the sight should fill me with an odd satisfaction. I marked her as mine.

I feed my cock into her inch by inch, but I feel aggressive. It is as if she's woken up some sleeping beast inside me. I want to slam into her and ride her until she screams. I want to see her submissive. I want to see her drink my cum. I want fill all her orifices with my cock. I want to possess her and own her.

"You can take all of me, can't you, baby?" I groan.

She spreads her legs wider and rocks her hips, as if begging me to do what I want. She has no idea how pretty her wet pussy looks when it begs like that. I slide back in, this time all the way to the root. Her eyes roll back in her head and I sweep my tongue into her open mouth, swallowing her cry of pain. When the pain eases, she pushes into me and grinds her hips, her pussy squeezing for all it's worth. I start thrusting harder, fucking in and out of her tight flesh. Our bodies rubbing against each other.

Less than five minutes. That's all it takes before her virgin pussy starts clenching and cumming on a cock for the first time. On *my* cock. I watch her with satisfaction. The way her body bows and her mouth opens in a cry of ecstasy. I don't want to come. Not yet. I'm not ready. I want to watch her break apart again. I grit my teeth when I feel the orgasm gather in my balls and try to think of something else, but there's no chance. I lose it and it happens. I join her in paradise. We become one long intense orgasm, one skin, one animal.

I had never had a sweeter fuck. It's so perfect, its beauty fucking kills me.

He kisses my throat, my chest, my nipples, my mouth while I fight to breathe normally. He is still inside my body and hard as a rock, filling me completely. Tears spring to my eyes, but I'm not in pain. It never crossed my mind that sex would be this incredible. When my body stops shuddering, I look up into his eyes. They are ablaze with naked lust. I feel as if I'm drowning in him, but that's all right. I want to.

"I didn't know what I was missing all this time," I whisper, shocked to my core.

"You think this happens all the time?"

I stare into his eyes. "It doesn't?"

'It's never been like this for me," he says softly.

"This must be how it's supposed to be. I feel connected, really connected, body and soul to you."

"You have no idea at all how damn beautiful you are, do you?"

I wriggle under him and his face changes. "God, being inside you feels so fucking amazing."

He grinds his pelvis against my clit and my mouth opens in a gasp of surprise at the shaft of pleasure that jolts into my body even though there is a small sweet ache there. "I don't think I can take anymore of you tonight," I groan.

"You will take more of me, and you'll love every second of it," he growls.

He pummels me. Harder, deeper, grunting a little. All I can do is whisper, "Yes, I love it … it's so good … more, more, please … yes, Tyson … yes … more …" His jaw sets firm and he stares deep into my eyes as he fans the flames of the fire he started in me. I gasp every time our bodies slam together and my gasps get louder as the tension builds and he pushes me higher and oh, my God, I come again, clawing at his shoulders, and give in to it, screaming as ecstasy rocks me to my core.

He lets go too, slamming into me until he collapses with a low growl.

"My God," he pants against my neck. I can only whimper in response. Then the room becomes quiet. Nothing but the sound of our heavy breathing filling the dark bedroom.

I wake up suddenly, my eyes flying open. I can see from the little slit in the black-out curtains that it is already morning. How the hell did that happen? The ribbons. Charlotte.

Shit! Shit! Shit!

I move and his arm comes around me. "Where do you think you're going, young lady?" he asks with a slow smile.

I can't hang around. "What time is it?" I ask, rubbing my eyes before I remember about smudging my makeup. What a mess I must look.

"Almost seven."

"Damn it! I can't hang around. I promised Charlotte I would go pick up her ribbons." I try to scramble out of bed, but he grabs me by the waist and pulls me back against his body. Talk about morning wood!

"Hang on," he whispers in my ear. "Let me take you … after your morning fuck."

"No, I don't have time for that," I wail, almost in a panic. Just because I found a man I won't let Charlotte down. We've been planning this day for months.

He gets up on his elbow, and looks down at me, all unshaven and sexy. "All right, we'll both get ready and I'll take you."

"No, you can't," I say gently. "This is Charlotte's day. She's the bride and the center of attraction. If I bring you back with me, I'll steal the limelight from her. She's my best friend, Tyson."

He frowns. "So you're just going to run out on me?"

"Uh … huh. Let's meet after the wedding. The cake cutting will be done by 5.30 and I can disappear as soon as Charlotte has changed into her going away clothes which should be about 6.30. Wouldn't it be terribly romantic if we meet in that cute Italian restaurant on the same street as Le Coq? I think it's called Basilico."

He shakes his head. "Basilico is not on the same street as Le Coq."

"Isn't it?"

"Nope."

"Oh, okay, I saw a Costa on that street. Let's meet there at 7pm, and then we'll go to the restaurant together. We need to talk."

"Sounds great. Off you go," he says and slaps my butt.

I scramble out of bed and streak stark naked to the bathroom. His laughter follows me and I try not to slam the door in my frenzy. Shit, I managed to smudge mascara all over my face back there. Smooth move. Five minutes and a lot of soap and hot water later, I run out into the bedroom wrapped in a towel. He's got out of bed and is waiting for me with my shoes in hand. He is also distractingly naked. In the morning light his cock is really, really big.

"Here you go." He smiles, but pulls the heels back before I can grab them.

"What is it?" I ask.

"Your face."

"Oh, what?" I touch my fingers to my freshly washed face. "I know I look horrible. You don't have to remind me."

He shakes his head. "You look even better without makeup on."

"You are such a liar," I accuse with a giggle as I grab for the shoes. "You already got me in bed, Tyson. You don't need to lay it on so thick."

"I mean it. Hey." He grabs my wrist and pulls me close, knocking the wind out of me when our bodies collide. "I do mean it. You look even more beautiful with no makeup and messy hair."

"Well ... thank you," I mumble, feeling like the world's biggest ass for giving him a hard time.

"What will you do today?" I ask.

His smile is warm and it fills my heart. "I was supposed to fly out last night, but I met a sweet blonde who turned my head so I'm here in Paris with nothing to do." He grins. "I have a friend who has a stable two hours from here. I'll spend the day with him. He has a mare that I'd like to buy."

"Right. So I'll see you this evening."

"Hey, before you go ..."

"What?"

"Show me your ass."

I blink hard, sure I must have misheard him. "Come again?"

He laughs, the sound warm. "I would love to, but I thought you were in a hurry."

My cheeks burn furiously. "Very funny."

"I mean it," he says softly, his eyes full of determination. "Show me your ass."

Slowly, I turn around.

"Lift your dress and bend over."

I obey, and when I turn around he is sporting an almighty erection.

He rewards me with a sweet, lingering kiss—I'm glad I rinsed with mouthwash a few minutes ago—before releasing me.

"Damn, I really need to run." I hurry to the door, grabbing for the purse I dropped when we got in.

"Take my number," he says.

He calls it out and I key it into my phone and start walking towards the door.

"Give me a missed call," he says with a smile. For a second I turn and stare into his eyes. At that time, it never even crossed my mind that we would not be together. I took for granted that we would meet and travel back to England together. How could we not be together? We were so perfect together. At that moment I was so naïve I forgot that he is not Mr. Commitment. That he fucks girls and forgets them the next day.

That he makes promises he never keeps.

# TYSON

I run my shaver down my cheek and can't stop grinning at my own reflection. I feel like the cat that ate *all* the cream when I remember how good it felt inside her, how eager she was for me. She was a virgin, but she was fucking fantastic in bed. The sex was, quite literally—mind-blowing, and I don't use that term. Ever. Just when I thought it couldn't get any better, it did. Much better. Shit, it's *never* been that good with anyone.

Yeah, she's something else.

Beautiful, funny, smart, a great dancer, and to top it all a heart of pure gold. I've known more than a few women who wanted to twist my stones because I wanted their bodies. When they landed on their ass outside my front door they found out: nobody has me by the short and curlies.

One thing for sure, she is the first woman I wished didn't have to leave in the morning. I'd been up long before her. I knew I should wake her so she could get to that wedding on time, but I found myself unable to do it. How could I? When she was this sweet, peaceful angel lying in my arms, a little satisfied smile on her face, and snoring softly.

For all that adorable snoring though, she must have a backbone of steel to have resisted all the men who must have tried over the years, plus the social pressures around her, and remained a virgin all this time. Maybe that's what is so fascinating about her. That unusual mixture of strength and vulnerability. I remember how she blushed when I called her beautiful. As if she didn't quite believe me. Could she be so totally unaware of her own beauty? Most women with half her looks would be strutting their stuff morning, noon and night. She's a breath of fresh air, for sure.

I realize I'm humming as I step into the shower. Since when do I hum? Then again, I'm never this damn happy. I'm so fucking happy I almost want to jump up and down on Oprah's sofa. How absurd is that? As I lather up I kinda wish I didn't have to wash the scent of her off my skin. I want to hold onto her for as long as I can, but life calls. The bizarre thought makes me laugh at myself.

I leave the bathroom and look at my phone. There is no missed call from her yet. Drying my hair with one hand, I open the photo I snapped of her at the club when she wasn't paying attention. She was looking down at the table, tucking a chunk of hair behind her ear, and I couldn't resist that unique aura of vulnerability and innocence around her.

Now I know why she looked innocent and fragile, but at that time, it intrigued me. Even now looking at her photo touches something in me and brings out my protective side. As if I need to shield her from the big bad world.

"What's with you, man?" I say aloud, shaking my head. I've

never been so soppy about a chick before. I click into my inbox. There's an email from Ralph, the head of my stable, asking why I didn't turn up last night. I fire back a quick reply, assuring him I'll be back in the next couple of days.

Thoughts of her race through my head as I get dressed. My gaze falls on the room service menu and I smile to myself when I remember the way she laughed over my room service misstep. She took it well, though. And she has a nice laugh. Sexy.

I call Louis and arrange to meet up for lunch. I look out of the window. It's a beautiful day. Instead of having breakfast at the hotel, I decide to walk over to the patisserie around the corner.

There are a few people standing in line at the bakery. A few of them look at me and I realize I must still be grinning to myself. It doesn't bother me that much. Getting stared at is not a new thing for me. The gossip rags are notorious for spotting me at my worst and screaming about it for the world to see and hear. I wink at an old lady in a black dress who seems unable to take her eyes off me. She smiles and says, "Le monde est un bel endroit quand tu es amoureux."

M y French is iffy at best, but it sounds like, the world is beautiful when you are in love.

I'm not in love, but hell it sure feels good. I grin at her and tell the server I want to pay for her stuff. She wags her finger knowingly and laughs at me as she leaves with her baguette and baked goods.

I get a sandwich and coffee and go back out into the

sunshine. The world seems beautiful. It's definitely a good day for a wedding. I wonder what Izzy is doing as I walk down the sideway. I know it's probably just an infatuation and it won't last. I'll eventually figure out she's just a normal woman with all the pitfalls of a normal woman, but for now she's all I can imagine wanting for the rest of my life.

I look at my watch. Less than eight hours before our date tonight. At this rate, I don't know how I'll be able to wait that long. I can't get her out of my head. Who'd have thought I would be actually looking forward this much to a night with a girl? Never happened before. I bite into my thickly filled baguette and I hope my concentration kicks in before I get to Louis's place, because right now I'm on Planet Izzy.

My phone buzzes and my first thought is: my missed call from Izzy, but when I see Liam's name on the ID, I smile … and the day just got better. It's like he knows when I need him to bounce off. He'll understand. I laughed at him when he got together with Vanessa, but he just smiled knowingly and said one day I'd understand. He's probably the only friend I have who would not take the piss out of me for getting hooked on a girl after one night.

I hit the green button on my screen. "You fucking fell off the face of the Earth, man. Where the hell have you been?" I ask with a laugh. I wait to hear his snarky comeback, but there isn't one. Instead, I hear a strange sniffling sound. "What's up, bro? Are you sick?" I ask warily.

"Tyson?" A woman's voice, thick with tears.

Just like that, my blood runs cold.

# IZZY

"Stop being so coy and bloody well tell us what happened last night," Lina demands.

The dressmaker is getting Charlotte into her meringue dress, a complicated affair with boning, petticoats, tapes and stuff so we're staying well clear and having a quick glass of champagne outside the bedroom.

"I had a great night," I say casually. "We went dancing to this really fun sixties club, then we ended up in his hotel room."

"Ended up in his hotel room? What the hell kind of story is that?" Catherine huffs. "We need details, girl. How many times? Positions? Length? Girth? You know, the usual works."

"Well, at least tell me the guy has a small dick," Kylie says, gulping down her champagne.

I smirk.

"What?" she explodes. "Are you telling me he is to-die-for good looking, rich, famous, and has a big dong too!" She shakes her empty glass at me. "I'll say this for you, Izzy Faraday. You sure know how to pick your one-night stands."

I frown. "It was not a one-night stand. We're meeting for dinner tonight."

Not only Kylie's but both Lina's and Catherine's jaw drop. "What?" all three cry in unison.

I had to pinch myself in the taxi because I simply couldn't believe what happened to me could be real so I totally get their surprised faces. "Yeah, we're meeting for dinner tonight," I say, and can't help feeling totally smug about it all. Tyson is so amazing. Everything had been so perfect.

"Are you guys going to date?" Lina asks in a shocked voice.

"I don't know." I shrug. "We didn't get a chance to talk much last night—"

"I bet," Kylie interrupts sourly.

"But I really hope we do. He's really special," I say ignoring Kylie's sarcastic comment. "Anyway, we're meeting for dinner to talk. He wanted to come for the wedding, but I didn't think it would be fair to Charlotte. It's her big day, and the last thing I wanted was to make it anything else but her day."

Catherine is the first to let out a whoop of joy. "That's incredible, Izzy. I mean, do you realize that you've hooked up with the famous Tyson Eden? The guy who's been voted by GQ as the number one guy you'd sleep with in secret, but wouldn't take home to meet mama."

I grin. 'Last night was perfect, Cat. Just perfect. It was everything I ever dreamed of."

Catherine grins back, genuinely happy for me. "I'm glad to hear that, honey. You deserve a good man."

"Be careful though. He's known to be a player," Kylie says.

"Stop raining on her parade," Lina scolds Kylie. "A man is a player until he meets the right woman. Look at Clooney. The guy was a confirmed bachelor until he met Amal."

"That reminds me. I should call him. He asked me to give him a missed call so he has my number too," I say, digging into my purse, my stomach lurching with fear. I search all round, then frantically pour the contents of my purse out, but my phone's not in it.

"Don't tell me …" Catherine says.

I look up at my friends with a frown. "I can't believe it. I've lost my phone."

"Where was the last time you had it?" Lina asks.

"I keyed in his number in the hotel room and remember putting it back into my purse in the elevator. I must have dropped it in the taxi." I pause. "Or maybe I left it at Monsieur Armand's shop when I went to collect the ribbons."

"You've got everything backed up, haven't you?" Cat says.

I nod. "Except his number."

"Can't you call him at the hotel?" she says.

"No, he said he was going to see his friend who lives two hours away about a horse."

"I don't think you should call him, anyway. You don't want to seem desperate," Kylie says.

Lina turns to Kylie. "Excuse me. Don't want to seem desperate? You'd have rung his phone five times by now if it was you."

"Never mind, I'll just see him tonight." I look at Catherine. "Do you think he will be upset that I didn't call?"

"Of course not. He will just assume that you were busy with the wedding. Talking of the wedding here comes Charlotte."

I turn towards the bedroom door and Charlotte is standing there with a horrified expression on her face. "I tore the veil," she wails.

We all rush towards her. It is only a tiny tear and Catherine who is a whizz with DIY stuff says she can repair it with a bit of glue. I run downstairs to look for glue. I will think about Tyson later.

# TYSON

"Vanessa?" I ask in disbelief. Only she would call from his phone ... and there's only one reason why she would call in tears.

"Yes," she confirms with a sniff.

'What's wrong with Liam?"

"First off I got to tell you that I'm going against Liam's wishes here. He didn't want me to tell you. We've argued about it numerous times. I've told him he should tell you, that you would want to know, but ..."

I grip the phone tight. "Tell me what, Ness? What is it?"

She lets out a choked sob. "I'm calling from the hospital, Tyson. Liam's been here for weeks."

"What?" It should have come out as a shout because there was a lot of emotion behind that word, but it exits as a horrified whisper.

"I'm so sorry. I wanted to tell you—"

"For what?" I manage to sputter.

"It's cancer, Tyson. They operated last night."

"What the fuck?" That comes out as a shout, shocking the people bustling around me. "Liam's got cancer? For how long?"

"He's known for six months."

"Six months!" I exclaim, utterly shocked. Liam is the only true friend I have. He's more like a brother. He'd have my back no matter what, and the same goes double for me. I'd do anything for him. And he didn't even want to tell me he has cancer. Cancer! Him? My head spins.

"Tyson, I'm sorry," she sobs brokenly. "I know it isn't right, and I told him so many times that you would want to know. That you deserve to, but ... he didn't want to see pity on your face. He didn't want anyone feeling sorry for him. And he knew you would, because you love him. I know you do."

"Oh, fuck," I whisper, stunned. He's twenty-six, just like me. People in the prime of life don't normally get cancer. That's for people who don't take care of themselves, the ones who smoke and drink too much, and eat food full of nitrates and shit like that. Not us.

"He knew there was nothing you could do for him. There was nothing any of us could do, believe me. I've been with him every day and I've never felt so helpless in all my life. Watching him waste away ..."

I shake my head, wishing I could make sense of the thoughts racing through it. Liam has cancer. He's dying. He's wasting away. And he didn't tell me. "You said there was an operation?"

She sniffles loudly. "The operation went all right, but something happened overnight. I don't know what, but since then he's been going downhill. They've been working on him all day. They can't tell what it is, but it seems like his body's just … I don't know, just shutting down. Tyson, please come. They don't think he'll make it past tonight." She breaks down then, sobbing horribly. I can't sob. I can't even muster a tear. I can't feel anything.

"I'll be on the first flight out," I promise.

"Please, hurry. I'll tell him you're coming. I know he would want to hold on for you, Tyson." I get the address. There's a fist squeezing my heart when I end the call. *Liam, you fucking idiot. How dare you not even give me the chance to help?*

I pull up a random travel site on my phone and search frantically for flights to Ireland—my fingers keep hitting the wrong buttons at first, but I eventually manage to schedule a flight going out in two hours. I buy the ticket on the spot and rush back to the hotel.

I rush up to my room and start throwing things into my suitcase, cursing him, mourning him, and wishing I could wring his fucking neck for being so stubborn and stupid. He is dying in some hospital bed in Ireland and there's nothing I can do about it. He should've known I would want to be there, the jackass. A lifetime of being my best friend and he thought it would be all right not to tell me he was fuckin' dying.

Suddenly, I remember Izzy.

"Damn it!" I whisper, running my hands through my hair. I look around, frantic, in a panic. I'm losing my fucking mind. I grab the phone that I tossed on the bed. I have to keep myself from hurling the damn thing to the floor when I see she still hasn't given me that missed call.

I pace my suite restlessly like a caged tiger.

She'll call soon. She's just busy doing whatever bridesmaids do. Fuck, what if she calls while I am airborne? I change the recorded message on my phone's answer machine. My message tells her that I have to fly to Ireland on an emergency and could she leave a number and I'll call her back.

Another thought hits me. What if she doesn't have the time to call and she is just planning on showing up in Costa tonight? Another thought hits me. Maybe she hasn't called me yet because she was in such a hurry to get her ribbons she made a mistake with my number.

In that case, she won't hear my message. She'll think I ditched her. That I was never serious in the first place. She was only a fling. I imagined her sitting there, waiting for me, hopeful. Until enough time passed and she knew I wasn't going to show. I could actually feel her pain as though someone were stabbing me.

The thought of hurting her is almost as crushing as the pain of my best friend dying. Like a knife to my heart. She doesn't deserve to be hurt like that, especially when hurting her is the last thing I want to do. It is at that moment I realize she's even more special to me than I had recognized.

I slump on the bed. I have enough time to leave her a message with the staff at Costa.

I snatch my suitcase, check out, and rush out of the hotel. Outside I flag down the first taxi that comes my way and direct the driver to the pub in question. While we're on the way, I call Louis to cancel my lunch with him, then I shoot emails to Ralph and several others, letting them know about the change in plans. Ralph gets back to me instantly, telling me he'll handle things on his end. He knows how much Liam means to me, the brother I never had.

"Wait here, please," I say when we pull up outside Costa. I fly through the door and up to the counter. I ask to speak to someone who can understand English.

One of the girls comes towards me from the other end of the counter. "Can I help you?"

"Yes, please. Will you be working here at about seven tonight?"

"Yes, I am working, how do you say, is it … double shift?"

I nod quickly.

"Yes, double shifts tonight."

"Good. I need you to do a big favor for me," I explain as I fumble with my phone, searching for Izzy's photo. "I'm supposed to meet this girl here at seven tonight, but I have to leave the country because of an emergency. Do you under-stand me?"

She nods. "Yes."

"I don't have her number. I need her to know that I'm not standing her up, right?"

"Ah, I understand." She smiles, a smile that tells me she understands and everything will be all right. "You want me to tell her you can't make it tonight because of an emergency."

Nodding, I smile back at her. The relief feels like physical sensation in my body. I exhale. Oh, thank God. She will look out for Izzy and tell her what happened. "Do you have a piece of paper I can use?" The guy behind the bar slides me a notepad and a pen.

I*zzy,*

*I'm so sorry, but there's been an emergency. My best friend is critically ill and I have to fly out a.s.a.p.*

*Please call me when you get this.*

*x Tyson.*

Underneath, I scrawl my cell number.

"Here." I hand it over to her. "Please, give this to her." I show her the photo again. "This girl."

"She's beautiful," she says.

"Yes, she is. Which is why I can't let her think I stood her up. This means the world to me." I pull out two hundred Euros and shove the bunch of notes into her hand. "Thank you."

"Sure, no problem!" she says, grinning from ear to ear. "I'll be here tonight, and I promise to give her this note. Actually, if you call here at that time I can even let you speak to her."

A great weight slides off my chest. It's not ideal, but it's the best I can do at the moment. "That would be wonderful. Thank you."

"No problem. When you call just ask for Margot." She grins. "That is me."

I smile at her gratefully. "You're a life saver."

"Good luck," she says as I turn away, clutching the notepad with the establishment's phone number.

As I walk out, I suddenly wish there was a way for me to take Izzy back with me. It seems wrong to leave her here, but I have no choice but to climb back into the taxi and tell the driver to take me to the airport. I get to the airport with just enough time to get through security and board the plane. As it takes off I look down at the earth below and my heart feels heavy with some unknown fear.

Izzy will be all right, I tell myself. She'll call soon and hear the message. She'll understand. I know she will. We have something special. Any other woman might think it was a brush off, but not her. She'll know there was nothing else I could do. I have to be with my friend—or at least try to help his girlfriend through the aftermath … if I don't make it there in time to say goodbye. He would do the same for me.

I can't wait around another day. I gave my word. And my word is always good.

# IZZY

https://www.youtube.com/watch?v=X930_IyhGfo
Dust to Dawn

I tap my nails against the glass of iced coffee. Condensation wets my fingers and runs down the side to pools in a ring around the glass. My eyes dart around—every movement on the street could be him. Every tall, dark-haired man makes me jump. Even the ones who aren't so tall, or so handsome. My heart still skips a beat whenever anyone who looks even remotely like him strides past the windows. Whenever the door opens I turn my head. It might be him. It just might be.

But it isn't.

I can just see the look on Kylie's face when I tell her I sat around in Costa, waiting for a man who clearly had no intention of ever seeing me again.

Yes, that would go over really well.

My chest hurts. A deep, stinging pain that only gets worse with every minute that passes. Every tick of the clock feels like another second of my life gone. Last night comes back to me like scenes on a reel of film. His smile. The way he looked at me. The way he laughed at himself. The electricity of his touch. The way my breath caught when he swept me off my feet—literally—and carried me to the bedroom. The look in his eyes when I woke up the next morning. The way my heart pounded double time when he told me he wanted to see me again.

The images play like a movie I can't stop. I wish I could stop it. It's hell—the memories don't bring pleasure or fill me with a secret joy like they did all day. Now they're a reproach. The reminder of what an idiot I was to believe him.

And yet, I keep hoping.

Craning my neck whenever the door opens. When it doesn't turn out to be him, my heart sinks further and further. I know I can't sit here all night, waiting, but … just a little while more.

As the night moves on I feel the eyes of the wait staff watching me, pitying me. They've probably seen dozens of girls like me, maybe hundreds. Walking in with their heads high, all dolled up in their best clothes, their hair and makeup much nicer than they'd wear it if they were meeting up with just friends. Checking their reflection, self-consciously looking up every time the door opens. Just about radiating anticipation.

Until enough time passes. Until anticipation turns to embarrassment, then despair. And all the while, they try to keep up a brave front because they are in public. They can't let anybody see them fall apart, even though falling apart is the one thing they are going through. What a pathetic fool I was to be roped in by a good-looking face.

I cringe to think that I was so easy.

The staff are roping off sections without customers. They are about to close shop. Some of them look in my direction. They want me to go.

The nasty, taunting voice in my head starts a monologue. *Kylie was right. What were you thinking? A man like him is not for you. This was bound to happen. Better now than later. It was just a one-night stand. It's life. Every night millions of men and women all over the world are doing it and walking away.*

I stand suddenly. I have to get out of here. My cheeks are burning, there's a tightness in my chest. It feels as if I'll explode if I stay here a second longer.

"Goodnight," one of the waitresses says as I walk to the door. There's sympathy in her eyes. Like she wants me to know I'm not the only one who's ever been through this. Strangely enough, my pride kicks in. I don't need her sympathy. I'm not hurt. So what if I made a complete fool of myself by sleeping with a man who is known to be a Casanova, and actually expected him to show up for lunch after he got what he wanted.

"It looks as though my meeting got canceled without my knowing about it." I manage to smile. "Goodnight."

She's diplomatic enough to pretend she believes me. Nodding politely, she walks away. Tears of shame burn behind my eyes. She knows. They all know. Thank god I'll never be coming here again. I hurry out, careful to avoid eye contact as I go. I wish I'd never come. I wish … God, I wish … I wish he had just turned up.

I can't go back to the apartment just yet. The thought of sitting with my friends for the rest of the night enduring their pitying glances … it's too much to even think about. How they will laugh at me. Saving my virginity all these years and dropping it into the lap of the worst kind of skirt-chaser. I look back and forth down the street. A taxi stops. I get in and to my shock I ask the driver to take me to his hotel.

I walk through the lobby, and up to the reception. A woman in a navy suit smiles professionally.

"I'd like to speak to Tyson Eden, please," I say, meeting her in the eye.

She frowns. "Monsieur Eden? I … um … let me check." She looks down at her computer screen and taps at a few keys. She looks up shaking her head. 'Sorry, Mademoiselle, but Monsieur Eden checked out this morning."

My eyes widen. "What?"

"Yes, he checked out at eleven o'clock." She shrugs. "Sorry."

For a second I stare at her blankly. He checked out. So even that story about going to see his friend was bullshit. My mind refuses to believe it. I cling on to the last bit of hope. "Did he leave a message for me?"

She shakes her head slowly, her eyes pitying. "No, sorry. He did not leave a message for anyone. If he had there would be a notice in the notes section."

I nod and, turning around, head out of the hotel. My mind is blank as I walk the streets of Paris for ages. Even when it starts raining I don't stop walking. There I was, thinking I was smart. I wouldn't ever get roped in by a handsome face or a charming smile. Holding myself above all the poor, silly girls who let men take advantage of them. What did I think made me so special, so smart? I was clearly wrong. I was wrong about so many things.

I think back to how happy I was only a few hours ago, how I spent the whole day smiling and giggling to myself like I was the keeper of the most wonderful secret in the whole wide world. I feel so lost and hurt. A single tear rolls down my cheek and I knuckle it away.

I stop at the corner to wait for traffic to rush past and it hits me that something might have happened to him. My breath catches. All these cars racing past. What if he got hit on his way to Louis? Or had an accident? Maybe I should call up the hospital to see if he was admitted? No, that's stupid. He checked out of the hotel. What if he had to go home for something, like an emergency? That's surely possible.

A tiny flicker of hope sparks to life in my heart, but I put it out right away. Then why didn't he leave a message for me at the hotel?

# TYSON

Izzy still hasn't called my phone. I flag a taxi and go straight to the hospital. By the time I reach Liam's bedside, running full-out from the second I cross through the entrance, he is still hanging on, looking worse than I've ever seen him, but alive.

"You think you'll get rid of me that easily?" he wheezes. I can barely hear him.

I run a hand over his mostly-bald head and force a smile. "Keep your smartass comments to yourself. Rest a little, eh?"

He shakes his head. His eyes burn as he looks up at me. "Fuck rest. I'll rest when I'm dead. Hit me with all you've got, you pussy," he whispers.

I pretend to chuckle, and he chuckles with me, but I see that even laughing exhausts him. My heart aches to see how he still wants me to think of him as a strong man. I hold his hand and he squeezes mine, but there is no power left in him. He is just a shell of the man I knew. I want to know why he didn't tell me. How he thought I would take it if I never got the chance to say goodbye. But none of that matters now. It would only take up the little time we have left together.

Vanessa comes in with fresh coffee. She's a mess—hair dirty, pinned up on top of her head. Eyes ringed with dark circles, cheeks sunken in. Clothes that look like she's worn them for days on end. Her nose is red and chapped. I have to admit, I never cared much for her. Never thought she was good enough for him. Seeing the way she's falling apart taking care of Liam, and knowing she could easily have walked away when she found out he was sick makes me regret the things I said about her.

"It all happened so fast," she whispers softly as she sits on the other side of the bed, close to him. "He started coughing for no reason. He felt fine otherwise, no fever or anything. Just that cough. Then, he lost his appetite. And he was tired all the time. I would say three or four weeks between when it started and when I managed to convince him to see the doctor."

"He always was a stubborn ass," I mutter.

"That's the truth," she agrees, shaking her head with a rueful smile. "But it was too late by then. The doctor said it was Stage Four lung cancer."

"How long ago was that?"

She looks up at the ceiling. "Three months?" she says with a shrug.

My hands clench. Three months. He could've gotten better treatment. He might have had a chance, but no, the stubborn bastard insisted on keeping it a secret from me and letting the cancer ravage him. My eyes find his face and I see the way it has eaten him out. His hair is all but gone, and his pallor is ghostly grey. Eyes and cheeks sunken like a survivor of a Nazi concentration camp. I can hardly believe this is the same man I used to sprint up and down the football pitch with. Somebody replaced my best friend with a withered old man.

"They must be able to do something for him."

She looks at me from across the bed. "Nothing we can afford. Nothing feasible."

"Afford? Feasible?" I hiss. Money? Is that all he lacked? When I have more of it than I'll ever know what to do with? I'd kill him myself if he wasn't already so close to it. The bastard.

She shrugs uncomfortably.

"I can afford it, Ness."

"He didn't want you to do anything like that," she says, her voice breaking. "He's proud and stubborn. He wanted it this way."

"How could he want this?" I ask, furious but trying to keep my voice down for his sake. What I want to do is punch a wall, curse him for being such an idiot.

"You know how he is," she says, like that's an answer.

I stand up. "Tough shit. He's going to have to deal with help from me. I can't accept this. I want to speak to his team of oncologists, immediately. I want to explore other alternatives."

"Tyson, no." She rises, grabbing my arm as I'm about to storm out the door and raise holy hell in the corridor. I look down at her, surprised. Why would she stop me from getting help for him?

She swallows hard. "If it's more of what he's had, no. You don't know how much he's suffered in the last three months. Believe me, there is nothing I want more than for him to be alive, to be with me, but I love him so much I won't put him through anymore. Enough is enough."

I touch her arm. "I'll find a way. A way where he doesn't suffer." My voice is strong and determined. "I need him. This is what I want. I can't sit here and not try, at least."

Her eyes swim with tears and a wild, crazy hope. "All right, then. Do it. I can't pretend I don't want you to do it."

He sleeps through the next few hours, and I sit up by his bedside. Just watching, waiting. Waiting for what? For him to open his eyes again? For him to die? The thought kills me and I walk out of his room and go down the corridor. There is a door that leads out to a garden. There is no one in it. There is still no missed call on my phone. I guess she must be so busy she is going directly to Costa.

I call Costa at eight sharp. A man answers on the first ring, and I ask for Margot. She comes on the phone and immediately recognizes me.

"Is she there yet?"

"No, she has not arrived."

"No problem. I'll call back in fifteen minutes. Ask her to wait for my call."

"Got it."

I call again. And again. And again. Fifteen minutes became every thirty minutes. But each time the answer is always the same. She has not arrived. Finally, the answer was different.

"I'm so sorry. She has not come and we are closing now."

My heart is so heavy, I can barely thank her for her trouble. *Oh, Izzy. Did I completely misjudge you?* No. I'm a pretty good judge of character. I didn't make a mistake. No one can pretend such innocence. I saw the blood. That wasn't a lie. We were so perfect. So happy. I try to think of anything she might have said that would give me a clue as where she could be.

Suddenly, crazy thoughts and images start appearing in my head. What if she met with an accident? What if she's lying in a hospital even now? I imagine her broken and bleeding.

If it weren't for Liam, I would have gone back to find her, but he needs me. His doctors are trying to find him a place at the Oslo Comprehensive Cancer Center in Norway. I need to be here to move quickly when they arrange something. My brother needs me.

I go back to Liam's room and he is still asleep.

"You look like shit. There's no need for both of us to be here. He'll sleep right through now. Why don't you take a break?" Vanessa says to me.

I rub the back of my neck. "Why don't you take a break? I'll stay with him."

She smiles. "I'll be all right. I'm happier when I'm here, next to him. You go ahead. There is a hotel just up the road. It's not much, but you'll be close by, and you can refresh and recharge. You're no good to him tired and irritable. Go on."

I don't want to leave the hospital, but the doctor assures me things look all right for now. I haven't slept in over twenty-four hours and Ness is right. Liam needs me at my best. I take a taxi to the hotel Vanessa told me about.

The room is drab and basic. I drop my bag on the bed and walk to the window. The hospital is so close by I can see from where I am standing. A square gray building. I think of all the people who work there, who die there.

I should sleep.

The bed looks comfortable enough, but when I lie down and close my eyes, all I see is Izzy. I can't get her out of my head. I roll onto my back with my arm over my eyes.

And there she is again.

# IZZY

I get lost in the maze of streets and don't even realize I am lost until two men walking towards me say something in French to me, but their body language and leering faces snaps me out of my daze.

I'm alone in a dark street with two men who look like thugs. I don't think I have ever been so frightened in my life. I drop my head and crossing the road start walking away quickly. My heart hammers in my chest. My ears listen for their footsteps. They don't follow. One of them laughs and calls something out. I don't turn. Just keep my head fixed straight ahead and my stride long and fast.

To my relief, only a short distance away, the street joins a busy one full of traffic and people.

I run the last few steps and burst on to the busy street. I look around me. I realize for the first time that I am soaked to the skin and shivering. Nobody takes any notice of me. I flag down a cab and give the address of the apartment I am staying in to the taxi driver.

He doesn't speak. Simply grunts, switches on the meter, and starts on driving.

By the time I get back to the apartment, everyone is asleep after all the champagne at the party, and only Marie, Lina's French friend, whose apartment we are staying in, is awake.

"You are wet," she says and shoos me towards the bathroom.

My mind is blank as I peel off my clothes and get into the shower. I don't even cry. Slowly, feelings come back to my frozen limbs. Eventually, I get out and wrap myself in the thick bathrobe Marie hung behind the door for me.

I dry myself and go into the living room where she is watching TV. To my surprise Lina has come to join her friend in the living room. They are talking in low tones. When they hear me they both turn towards me, but it is only Lina who speaks to me.

"I heard the doorbell. What are you doing here?" she asks, a frown on her face.

I shake my head, because quite honestly, I cannot speak. Cannot say a word. She stares at me for a few seconds then, she stands, and comes over to me. "Come on, let's have a cup of tea in the kitchen."

We go into the kitchen, but it is not tea she takes down from the cupboard, but a bottle of cognac. I sit down and watch her pour a generous measure into two mugs. I smell the fumes from where I am sitting. I drank Jameson last night. I can still taste it on my tongue.

She pushes one of the mugs towards me. I curl my hands around it and drink it down. All of it in one go. It burns my throat and makes me cough. I look at Lina's face.

Her mouth quirks. "It's okay, honey. It happens to all of us."

I bite my lip. She doesn't understand, but I nod. I can't talk about it. Not to her. Not to anyone. She can never understand. No one can.

"So Charlotte went on her honeymoon. Everything went really well," she says softly.

I nod.

"Kylie got really drunk and threw up in the toilet," she adds into the awkward silence.

I nod again.

She drinks her cognac and refills our mugs. I drink it and stand up.

She stands too. "I'm really sorry, Izzy."

I nod, then I turn to leave.

"I'm here if you need to talk," she says.

I turn. Her face is soft and full of concern. I nod and manage a half-smile. For the first time in my life, the pain is too deep for me to talk about my pain to anyone.

Tyson

"Norway?" Vanessa chews on her lower lip, looking uncertainly from me to Liam and back to me.

Liam frowns. "Why?" he whispers weakly.

"Because there are specialists there who are in the middle of developing a new treatment for your specific cancer. There are doctors throwing all their expertise behind it," Liam's doctor says.

"Can he manage a trip like that?" Vanessa looks at the small team of doctors gathered at the foot of the bed.

"Yes. Mr. Eden has already made the arrangements for transport. All the necessary medical equipment can be taken onboard."

"And it's ready to leave whenever you are," I finish, looking down at my friend. "All you have to do is stop being a stubborn jackass and accept the very thing you would do for me if you were in my shoes."

"How much is it going to cost?"

"I can afford it," I say.

"No, it's too much," he protests.

"Stuff it. It's not too much. It's nothing." I touch his shoulder —it's like touching a skeleton. "Please."

Liam looks at Vanessa, his jaw set hard.

Her eyes fill with tears. "Please, Liam. Do it for me."

It's what decides it for him. "All right. Let's go to Norway."

# IZZY

Two Days Later

The journey back is strange and strained. I find it difficult to talk to the others and spend most of it pretending to be asleep. Lina's brother comes to pick us up.

As soon as he drops me off on my street, I wave goodbye to everyone and run up the three flights of stairs to my little apartment. I lock the door behind me, then lean against it. A strangled sob bubbles up out of my throat. I'm alone, finally. I can let it all out. Tears overwhelm me as I slide down the door and end up in a heap on the floor.

What's wrong with me? Why does it matter so much? He was just a man, just a man, just a worthless man. I made a mistake. So what? I had fun, right? Then why is my heart breaking? It must be my pride that's hurt. Yes, that must be it. My pride. My pride is hurt.

Though I did think we had something special. Nobody can tell me that night was not special.

I cry my heart out. When I finally manage to get myself up off the floor I feel cold determination take over. I'll get over this. I take my shoes off, then the belt of the brand new dress I wore for the first time today, a cute little knit dress that hugs my body and whose light grey shade complements my eyes. I pull it over my head and toss it on the bed, not even bothering to put it away.

I only wore it because I was sick of Catherine and Lina looking at me as if I was going to slit my wrists.

A pair of tracksuit bottoms and a cuddly old night shirt will suit my mood a lot better. I pull my hair into a bun on top of my head and put the kettle on. An afternoon of trashy TV is what I need more than anything. I'll get over you, Tyson Eden. You'll see, I'll get over you if it's the last thing I do.

# TYSON

Two Weeks Later

"It's looking good, Ralph. He's looking real good," I say into the phone. The Norwegian sky is a clear blue and the air is fresh and clean.

"That's great news," he says, and I can hear the smile in his voice. "Did they say when he can come home?"

"Not sure yet. They'll probably want to keep him around a few more days for observation, just to be sure he keeps improving. The trip out here wasn't easy on him, so he's got to be a little stronger first."

"That's understandable. And how are you holding up?"

That's out of character for Ralph. I can count on two hands the number of times he's asked me a question like that in the ten years we've known each other. Not that he doesn't care—it's that he doesn't know how to show it.

"I'm fine."

"Fine? Bull. Keep up the pace you're setting, and you'll be the one in hospital."

"This is not about me, Ralph."

"The doctors know what they're doing, Ty. Take a little time to yourself, get some rest."

"You don't know that I'm not getting any rest," I argue.

He chuckles. "You act like we've never met, like I haven't known you for ten years."

"What the hell does that mean?"

"It means that when you make up your mind to do something, you go all-in without taking anything else into consideration. That sort of focus is good when it comes to business, and it's why you're as good as you are at what you do, but you can't forget about yourself right now. Your burning the candles on both ends. Your life can't stop indefinitely."

"It won't be much longer. Only a few days, and we'll fly back."

"All right," he says, sounding unhappy. That's not something I can concern myself with right now. It's not like it's the first time I've made him unhappy with me. His disapproval is something I've learned to take in my stride.

Liam is sitting up in bed when I get back to his room, which is more like a hotel suite. Every aspect of our time at the clinic has been beyond my wildest hopes. He's put on weight. His color is better. He even has the energy to move around using a walker, though he doesn't move very far. Still, it's progress. I only wish Vanessa could've come with us, but she couldn't spend much more time away from work. She'll be that much more surprised when we get home.

"How's Ralph?" he asks with a smile.

"The same as always and dead chuffed to hear you're doing so well."

"For once, I can say you were right about something," he admits with a wry grin.

"For once?" I raise an eyebrow, and we both laugh.

Then he looks troubled when the laughter fades. "I can't let you pay for all this without accepting something in return." He motions around us—the spacious suite with its view of a crystal-clear lake. "This is like a spa. And the treatments? All that cutting edge gene therapy and all these drugs they're pumping into me? I can't begin to imagine how much this is putting you out."

He's right about it being expensive. It's jaw-droppingly, obscenely expensive, but I would do it all again in a heartbeat to know my friend is improving. I smile at him. "I've never found anything more worth spending my money on than getting you well enough to break my balls and be a general pain in my ass. Sadly, I can't think of a single thing I'd rather spend my money on."

He opens his mouth and I raise my hand warningly. "End of discussion."

Three days later and we're back in Ireland. The reunion between him and Vanessa leaves me feeling a little misty-eyed. I've set him up with an in-house nurse so he can receive round-the-clock assistance, though at the rate he's improving I doubt he'll need it for very long.

When I think back only a few weeks ago and remember how close to death he was, it's enough to make me believe in miracles. There are no guarantees as to how long he has—but none of us have a guarantee, do we?

I almost believe I'll be able to find Izzy again, too. If Liam can have a turn around like this, anything's possible. Once I'm back in England in a few days, I'll start the process of finding her. There's got to be a way, even if I have to take out full-page spreads in every London paper until she notices. A good private investigator should do the trick, though.

"I'll see you tomorrow, brother," I tell him once he's settled in. Vanessa has hugged me at least ten times since we arrived, and she hugs me once more before I go.

"None of this would've been possible without you," she weeps against my shoulder.

"I'm just glad you called."

I fly back to England. I get out from the shower and go to sleep. My phone jerks me out of a deep, dreamless sleep. It's Vanessa. I experience déjà vu for the first time in my life.

"Hurry. They've taken him to hospital," she gasps into the phone. I sit bolt upright in the pitch darkness, dazed and still half-asleep.

"What? Why?" I scramble out of bed and pull my clothes together.

"I don't know! He wanted a nap. When the nurse tried to wake him for his meds, he wouldn't wake up!"

"I'll be there as soon as I can." It can't be true. It can't be. He was doing well. He had a second chance. There has to be some explanation, something stupid none of us thought of. A reaction to something. The doctors will be able to reverse it. They have to.

They don't. He never wakes up again.

# IZZY

## HTTPS://WWW.YOUTUBE.COM/WATCH? V=S43SPTUWKVA

*Never Give Up*

Charlotte's honeymoon is over. I've been expecting her phone call, but when my phone rings, I jump. The sun is low in the sky and I'm surrounded by balled-up tissue.

"Jesus, Izzy, Lina just told me what happened. Why didn't you tell me?"

"And spoil your honeymoon. Look, I'm all right now. It was just a one-night stand."

"Sweetie, I'm bringing over a bottle of wine. We'll get a takeaway."

One look at the mess around me and I have to object. "I don't know ..."

"It's not up for debate, cupcake. I'll be over in a flash." I know better than to argue with her. She always gets her way. I force myself off the couch and start tossing handfuls of used tissue into the wastebasket. I clear away the pizza boxes and the Chinese food takeaway cartons.

When I step into the bathroom to wash my face, the sight of my reflection makes me wince. The puffy eyes, the red, swollen nose. All this over a one-night stand. What an idiot. I splash cold water again and again in the hopes of bringing down the swelling and making myself feel a little more human. He's just a man. Just a silly man.

Charlotte agrees with me as she opens the first bottle of wine only minutes later. "He's just a man, like so many other men. Nothing special."

"I guess so," I say with a shrug, careful to avoid eye contact as I open boxes of good smelling Italian food. It occurs to me that I haven't eaten since breakfast, and my stomach rumbles in appreciation.

"You guess? Was he really that good?"

"Charlotte, please."

She swings her auburn hair over one shoulder and fixes me with a steady gaze. "Izzy, be honest with me. Are you really that broken-hearted over him?"

"I … no … yes, I am."

"Oh, sweetie." She rises up and, coming to sit next to me, pats my knees. "It'll pass. I promise you that. One day, you'll find the right guy and you'll look back on this time and be glad it was not him."

"Thanks."

She sighs. "I hate to see you hurt. You are such a sweetheart, you don't deserve this."

"For what it's worth, I hate it, too," I say with an attempt at a smile. "I just wonder if I did something wrong, is all. Did I fuck it all up?"

"Sweetie, you didn't do anything wrong. He was just not the guy for you. The most important thing is you enjoyed your first time. Some relationships are over in a night. They come, they go, but they have a purpose. You needed to throw caution to the wind and enjoy yourself. Which you did. Maybe that's all it was ever meant to be."

I wish I could believe that, but my heart tells me otherwise. How can I explain it to her? The way I felt when our eyes met. Like I understood him better than anybody else. His sense of beauty, his sense of what really mattered in life. There was a depth to him that I could see. And he saw something in me I don't think any man ever has. At least, that was how it felt. Perhaps the alcohol made me see things that weren't really there.

"I shouldn't have slept with him," I mutter.

"But then you wouldn't even have a good time to look back on. Do you know how lucky you are that your first time was so amazing, with such an experienced man? Most of us have to put up with a fumble and a poke in the dark," Charlotte reasons. "One day you'll look back on it and be glad that it happened the way it did. Believe me. You'll come to appreciate the memory. You said it was incredible, right?"

A sigh escapes me. "Yeah, it was."

"Accept that. And accept that you were two ships passing in

the night. You'll move on, and maybe you'll be a little wiser. You won't equate great sex with great love." She touches her wine glass to mine. "And let's not forget something."

"What's that?"

She smirks. "He doesn't know what he's missing, the daft prick. His loss."

I can't smile back. She doesn't understand. It's my loss. My loss.

# TYSON

https://www.youtube.com/watch?v=fkLUBxLMMio
Too Much

It's a cold day. Clear, beautiful. Almost like a spring day, come to think of it.

The sounds of weeping grow fainter, fainter, as the rest of the mourners file away from the gravesite. It's just me, hands clasped behind my back, standing in the middle of the church cemetery, looking at the casket that holds my best friend's body. I feel like I've aged ten years since that first call from Vanessa. He managed to linger another two days after he went to sleep, but that was the best he could do.

I stare at the polished casket. Why bother making it so shiny when it's only going into the ground? I walk up to it. Kneeling next to it, I rest my forehead against the shiny wood. He's in there. I close my eyes.

"Everybody thinks I care about the money, like it all went to waste because you died anyway, but you know what? I don't give a shit about it. I would have spent everything I have for you. If my money had kept you alive for one hour more, it was well spent. So those three weeks ... well, that's better than nothing. I got to tell you what needed to be said, and that has to be enough."

My voice breaks. I pause.

"Maybe I shouldn't have gotten all our hopes up. I don't know. It felt like the right thing to do at the time. I still don't know how it happened—maybe none of us ever will. Maybe that's the way it's supposed to be, but I fucking hate it."

I stand up and look down.

"You'll always be my brother," I choke out before turning away and walking down the gravel path leading to my car. I drive straight to the airport. My lawyers have already set up an investment fund for Vanessa. She never needs to worry about her old age or pension again. It was the least I could do. Her selfless loyalty to Liam touched me, and I know it would have made Liam happy to know she was taken care of.

Now, it's time to go home. Time to find Izzy. It is the only thing that will take my mind off the grief—and the feeling that I failed him.

# TYSON

## TWO YEARS LATER

https://www.youtube.com/watch?v=lnRS3A_ilYg
Pretty Woman

Fuck these early morning meetings. The negotiation went well, but having to deal with people first thing in the morning just kills my day. I smile to myself as I get off the elevator of the offices of my latest clients, or soon-to-be clients. They haven't signed on the dotted line yet, but they will. I can always smell the excitement of a buyer who is desperate for my horse, but thinks that playing it cool is a good strategy to lower my price.

Sometimes, I want to save them the trouble and tell them I never lower my asking price. I know what I'm selling. It's worth everything I ask for and more. But other times, I just sit back and watch the drama. It's a game they love to play. Those stingy bastards would ask for a discount on a bag of fries if they could.

If it weren't so ungodly early in the morning, I'd go out for a little celebratory drink. Instead, I need to find somewhere to pick up some chow. I missed breakfast and I'm starving. I know there's a little hole-in-the-wall café at the end of the next block that do huge fry-ups, so I head in that direction. It's cold and all around me people in thick coats are hurrying to the next warm place. Not me. I'm in a T-shirt. I love the cold. I even ride bare-chested in the middle of winter.

I open the door and the smell of coffee and grease hits me. My stomach rumbles.

The place is small and cozy and boiling hot. It has a hearth along one wall where people can curl their hands around steaming mugs of hot cocoa or coffee and chat quietly. There are two girls there right now, and they look me over with appraising eyes. There was a time, long ago, when I would have flirted right back. Not anymore. I've lost my mojo. Not even a lap full of gorgeous blondes could do it for me last week.

It's fairly crowded, but I find a table by the window and sit down. A waitress stops by. Her hair is tied back in a messy bun and she looks harassed. I order coffee, the With Everything On It Breakfast, and extra toast.

She nods and makes a note on her order pad. "You're hungry. Want black pudding on the side? It's good."

She just earned herself a hefty tip right there. "Why not?"

"Great. Be right back with your coffee," she says flashing a big smile.

I scan the place and people are turning around to watch me. Two years ago they would have turned to look at me because

I was a celebrity. Now it's because I'm a strange fucker with a big beard and long hair. If someone looks at me it's only because I'm so damn big and bearlike. Ignoring them, I take out my phone. I have one more appointment then I can get back on the road.

Truth is, I can't wait to get back to the farm, back to my horses. Dealing with horses is a lot less complicated than interacting with people. Something changed in me when I lost my friend. I understood in a real and material way that life wasn't endless. I had an expiration date. I lost my taste for the life I used to live, always needing excitement, getting into trouble, getting my picture in the gossip mags. But all that seemed like a waste of time.

Then once it became clear I was not going to be able to find Izzy, life lost all its color and vibrancy. I felt cheated by life. Everything I loved, wanted, was taken away. I devoted my time to my horses and I became a recluse and a workaholic. Some might even call me obsessed and a little mad.

There's a little old-fashioned bell above the front door and it tinkles whenever somebody comes in or goes out. It rings and my eyes dart up from my phone purely out of reflex. And what I see knocks all the air from my lungs.

Izzy.

I stare at her, frozen, disbelieving, mesmerized. The one person I've always hoped to see and the last person on Earth I ever expected to see again. The amount of times I've run up to a woman and turned her around only to be disappointed is too numerous to be counted. It never occurred to me that I would see her here in my old haunt. Especially after both the highly recommended private investigators I hired independently informed me they didn't even believe she lived in London anymore.

But here she is, right in front of me, smiling politely, holding open the door for a lady leaving at the same time as she is trying to come in. When the woman goes past she comes inside. Stripping her leather gloves off she rubs her hands together and blows at them through pursed lips. My astonished eyes follow her as she walks up to the counter.

How many times have I imagined seeing her again?

How many times have I dreamed this moment?

But by God, she makes all my dreams and fantasies seem like faded photographs. I stare at the color in her cheeks, the apple green of her eyes, the blonde strands of hair that have slipped out of her beanie hat. She is like an angel.

I never believed in miracles before, but this is just too incredible not to be one. What are the chances of running into her in a city of nearly nine million people? The sheer wonder of it gets me out of my chair and sends me over to her. She's standing in line, presumably to get a cup of coffee to go.

"Izzy," I murmur, standing behind her.

# TYSON

She jumps and whirls around, her eyes wide with shock. She's lost weight. At first there is just shock and surprise. Then she looks into my eyes…and recognition. For a fraction of a second I see a flash of a terrible, terrible mixture of sadness and longing. It's only there for a split second, but I know the look because I've seen it in my own reflection whenever I catch sight of myself thinking of her. The longing. Wondering what might have been.

Then, her eyes go ice cold. She might as well be looking at a lifelong enemy.

I ignore that. "It's you. I can't believe it's you. Out of the entire city …"

She nods, eyes moving over my face. "Small world and all that." There's something missing from her voice. Warmth. There's no warmth. She sounds defeated.

"Look. I can imagine how you must feel about me," I begin. I called the hotel I was staying at in Paris and the receptionist told me a blonde woman had come looking for me the night I checked out. I knew then she must have had a good reason for not calling me, or turning up at Costa that night. I was furious with myself for not thinking of leaving a message for her at the hotel. At any other time, I would have thought of it, but then with Liam on my mind I guess I wasn't thinking clearly. I've never forgiven myself for that. Never.

Her expression doesn't change. "No. You can't."

I look over her shoulder—there's nobody left in line. "Come have a cup of coffee with me. Just a few minutes. Please."

"I'm actually in a hurry." She takes a step away from me, then another. No. I can't let her get away that easy.

My hand shoots out, curls around her arm. She's definitely lost weight. "Please. Just a few minutes. Just once, so I can explain what happened."

One eyebrow rises. "There's an explanation?"

"Of course."

"I suppose you've had enough time to think one up." She glances over her shoulder, where a girl is waiting behind the counter to take her order. I realize I'm holding my breath, waiting to see what she'll do.

"Come on. What can it hurt to hear me out?"

"I'll take a latte," she tells the girl, then, she looks at me. "And I'll be sitting with this *gentleman*." There is sarcasm in the way she said the word gentleman, but my body sags with relief at her announcement. I lead her to the table and she sits opposite me, her spine ramrod straight.

"So what are you doing here?" She tucks her purse between

her body and the wall and lays her leather gloves on the table. Her left hand is empty—I have to stop myself before I pump my fist in the air. Not even engaged. Is it possible that she's been thinking about me these last two years, the way I have?

"I had a meeting with a potential buyer, just a block from here. I thought I'd stop in for a bite before heading back. I'm staying at a hotel nearby."

"I guess it's lucky you came in," she murmurs. She won't stop fidgeting. Her fingers drum on the tabletop. She keeps craning her neck to look up and down the street. What's she so nervous about?

"From where I'm sitting, yes. It's very lucky." I reach for her hand to quiet the drumming. She pulls it away like my touch burns.

She gives a nervous, breathy laugh. "It's been a long time, hasn't it?"

"Two years."

"Yes. Almost exactly."

"You look wonderful," I say softly, drinking her in with my eyes. She's thinner, but even more beautiful than I remembered her. Memory's a funny thing—it tends to paint a prettier picture than ever existed in reality. Not in her case. If anything, her hair is even more golden, her eyes a deeper green. Her skin is porcelain. Her lips are full, parted. I know what they feel like. She bites down on her lip and blood surges into my cock, making it twitch and thicken. Good thing there's a table blocking her view.

"Thank you." Her cheeks flush, making her even more

delectable. Almost like a doll, but a very passionate one. I've never forgotten the passion she showed me that night. I've never been able to find it anywhere else, in anyone else.

I can't sit here and make small talk anymore. "I feel like I owe you an apology or an explanation," I blurt.

She shrugs. "No, you don't. It's been a long time. A lot of water has passed under the bridge."

What happened to her? That's not what I expected—especially the attitude, the almost bored tone of her voice. Either she had never really cared or I'd hurt her so badly, she was putting on an act. Could her pride still sting after two years? "Then please, do me a favor and let me explain for my own sake."

"All right. Go on then." The waitress brings her latte and puts it in front of her. She looks up and thanks the woman. Her hand shakes when she picks up her glass of coffee. That gives me hope. She is not as unaffected as she pretends to be.

"For starters, it was stupid of me not to get your phone number right away. I can't tell you how stupid I felt when I realized we hadn't exchanged them. It wasn't deliberate, believe me. You were in a hurry and I was ... well, I was so happy I wasn't thinking clearly," I admit.

"Yes, you did want my phone number," she whispers, frowning.

"Oh, god, yes. Of course I did. I asked you to give me a missed call remember? You never did and I didn't know how to contact you."

She nods, a sad, faraway look in her eyes. She must be remembering that day.

"Anyway, after you left, I got a phone call. My best friend's girlfriend called me. He was dying back in Ireland. The doctors didn't even think he would make it past the night. He was the only brother I ever knew. We grew up together, went through everything together." I can talk about it without the hurt choking me anymore. There was a long time when I couldn't. "He had cancer. Lung cancer, and he never told me because he didn't want to ask for my help. I had to fly to Ireland. I had to help him."

Her frown deepens. She stares in my eyes, her gaze searching. She doesn't know whether to believe me or not.

"I still remember charging around my hotel room, wondering how to contact you so I wouldn't have to wait. I left a note there for you with a waitress in Costa. When you didn't show up ..."

Her head jerks back. "But I did show up."

It's my turn to frown. "No way. I called five times. You never showed up."

"That's impossible. I waited until closing time." She's still unsure, though. I don't blame her. It all sounds ridiculous.

Then it hits me. Oh fuck. "Which Costa did you go to?"

"I ... uh ... couldn't remember the name of the street, so I told the taxi driver the Costa on the same street as Le Coq club."

I close my eyes. It was that simple all along. "There are two Costas on that road. You said the one we passed."

She leans back, pale, sad. "I didn't know there were two Costas."

I cover her hand with mine. "Why didn't you give me a missed call?"

She shakes her head as if to clear it. "I lost my phone in the cab."

"Why couldn't my private investigators find you anywhere, not even on Facebook?"

"I don't use it much anyway, and if you were looking for an Izzy you wouldn't have found me. I'm registered under my full name, Isabella Faraday."

"All these things couldn't keep us apart. We ended up here together today," I say in wonder.

She frowns.

"Oh, Izzy. You have no idea how long and hard I looked for you."

"You did?" Her eyes are enormous. We stare at each other. Then something happens to her. A mask comes over her face. "What happened to your friend? Is he all right now?" Her voice is still shaky, but her face is still, composed; that of a stranger.

"I took Liam to Norway to a specialist hospital. Some kind of DNA mapping treatment. We spent more than two weeks there while he received treatment. He did well—very well. The tumors started shrinking and he made a tremendous turnaround. Energy, weight, appetite, it all started coming back, but it didn't last."

"Oh," she breathes.

"I'll never understand what happened. Sometimes I think it

might have been better for him and Vanessa if I had never stepped in. Better for me, too. Hope can hurt. It fucking crushed us. We had such hopes when he started coming around. So when he died anyway ..."

"I'm very sorry to hear that," she says. "Truly, I am."

I stare into her green, green eyes. She's just as beautiful as ever. Maybe more. Maybe it's two years of wanting that makes her look even better than I remembered. "I never forgot you, Izzy. A day didn't pass without me thinking of you."

Her eyelids flutter down. "It doesn't matter now."

I frown. "I want you to know I'm sorry you thought I stood you up, that I never cared. I did care. It ate my heart out, knowing you went to the hotel. I left a message at Costa, but with the shock of Liam's illness, I just never even thought about the hotel ..."

She holds up a hand and closes her eyes. "Don't, all right? Just don't."

"I'm not trying to dredge up old hurts—"

She opens her eyes and they're hard, cold. The way I've never seen them. "But you are. You are. Right now, you are." She leans forward. "I've gotten past it. Truly. It's not the same as it used to be. I don't feel angry or hurt. And now that you've explained yourself I understand the situation better. It's good ... having closure."

"Closure? What the fuck are you talking about?"

"I never understood what happened and now I know."

I wait for more. Nothing more comes. "And that's it? That's all you have to say?"

She blinks once, twice. "Why should I have anything to say?"

I have to admit, she has me at a complete loss. I watch her face and hope for some sign of encouragement. Anything to hang onto, work with. "I've never stopped thinking about you. Did you never think of me?"

She looks down at the table. "I've never stopped thinking about you, either."

Yes. I knew it. "You mean that?"

A casual shrug—or a shrug that's meant to look casual. "Of course. I wouldn't say it if I didn't mean it."

"Then you can't pretend that being here with me doesn't mean anything to you. That Fate bringing us together like this doesn't mean anything."

"It does mean something. It was horrible when I thought I had misjudged you. That you never meant to meet up with me. That you had gotten what you wanted and were moving on. That you didn't know how to let me down easy back at the hotel." She shrugs. "It took me a long time to get over you. Then I grew up. I appreciated that it was just part of life. Hurts that we have to go through to become the people we are. It's all in the past now. I'm sorry things turned out the way they did, for you, your friend, and us, but that's the way it was. We can't change anything now."

I watch closely. She can't mean it. It's not in the past. I refuse to accept the idea that we didn't run into each other to give us the second chance we deserve.

The bell on the door tinkles and she jumps, her eyes flying to the door and again I see the unguarded fear in her eyes, but it disappears so fast it is almost as if I imagined it. You can't work with horses and not have great intuition. Something is not right. I wonder who or what makes her so afraid?

# IZZY

https://www.youtube.com/watch?v=wzIE3mRFypQ
*Baby Can I Hold You Tonight?*

I can barely hear him over the sound of my own blood rushing in my ears. My heart is pounding so hard it is like a drum in a marching band.

Why did he have to come back into my life?

I don't need this complication. For two entire years, I've gotten by without him. I don't need him. I don't want him, but my palms are sweating and I can't get my heart rate under control. Something else too. Butterflies. Hundreds of them in my stomach. Making me feel nauseous with anxiety. I should leave. He is so big and distinctive. Anyone could see me here.

"Izzy ..." he calls urgently.

I look up into his eyes. I can stand sitting here across from him as long as I'm not looking in those impossibly blue eyes. They're just as beautiful as I remember, but there is something else in them. A bitter sadness. A sadness that makes me want to hold him close and rock him as if he was my baby. It isn't right for us to sit together the way we are.

It definitely isn't right that I feel exactly the same right now about him as I did when we first met—only now, I can't blame the giddy, dizzy feeling, the breathless excitement, on alcohol. Worse, I can no longer hate him for taking advantage of me, of being a coward and a user of the worst kind.

He will never know how difficult it is for me to shake my head and say, "It doesn't matter. Life has moved on for both of us. We're not those people anymore. I'm not that girl anymore."

"I don't believe you." His voice is soft, low, but deadly serious.

I wish he would. It would make things so much easier. His food arrives, but he doesn't touch it. He just keeps on staring at me.

"That's too bad. Because it's the truth." I shift in my chair, suddenly extremely uncomfortable. I've never lied to him before. Also, I've been sitting here too long. I look out the window again, just to be sure nobody's watching. The coffee sours in my mouth.

"Why do you keep looking out?"

I whirl my head around. "Because I'd rather be out there than here, with you."

"That's a lie, too."

"Don't call me a liar," I warn, my voice unsteady.

"But it is a lie," he says calmly. "You don't mean it. You want to be with me just as much as I want to be with you. I can feel it, and fuck anybody who says different."

I bite my lip, angry with myself for being so transparent. "You're so full of yourself. Doesn't it hurt, being that full of yourself?"

"It'll stop hurting when I'm inside you."

My mouth opens in a gasp of shock. I can put on a show to everyone else, but I can't try to hide the desire his words produce in me, there is no hiding from him. He could see right through me. From the very first moment we met.

Desire and dread fight back and forth in my heart. I don't know which is winning, but I don't wait to find out. I stand so fast I almost knock the chair backward. He stands too, his movements quick as a cat.

"I need to go now. Please, please don't follow me."

I leave the coffee and hurry to the door before he can stop me. I need to get out of here. I can't breathe. I can't think straight. For a second there, it almost seemed like a good idea to let myself fall for him again. He's tempting. As tempting as the Devil himself, but that would have been the worst mistake imaginable.

I'm halfway down the street, rushing and weaving between people casually strolling along, when I hear him calling to me. "Izzy! Izzy, wait!"

Shit, I can't have him following me and yelling for me like that. He must be crazy. Just to stop him from shouting my name, I come to a halt and whirl around. He's running, holding out one hand. He comes to a stop in front of me.

"Please, leave me alone."

"You forgot your gloves." He holds them out.

I take them from him, feeling confused and saddened. He only ran after me to return my gloves. I shouldn't feel sad. I can't have him, anyway. I take the gloves from him. "Thank you. I love these gloves." I tuck them into my purse rather than put them on. "And thank you for explaining what happened. I hope it's made you feel better. It's definitely made me feel a lot better." He doesn't say anything so I plough on. "Right. So I'll be off. I really have somewhere else I need to be."

"You can bullshit yourself, but not me. You gave up the most precious thing a woman can give, and you gave it to me. That means something. Nothing can ever change that. There is nowhere else you need to be but with me. Now." He takes a step closer and I know I should push him away. I need to. I ought to. But I don't. I let the magnetism of him pull me in all over again.

"Please, don't do this." It comes out as a weak, pitiful whisper.

"Come with me."

I shake my head. "I can't."

His smile is just as bright as I remember it, just as sexy, and warmer than the sun. It warms me from the inside out. "Yes, you can. You know you want this as much as I do. We deserve this. Both of us."

He is another step closer to me. I feel his warmth and smell his cologne. I want to fall into his arms here and now and never leave. What is the spell he has on me? I wish I could break it.

"I shouldn't …"

"You should, and you will." He is inches from me and I'm drowning in his eyes. I can't breathe. There's nothing in the world but him—nothing at all. Him and me. *Just this once, Izzy. For everything you have suffered.*

I'm in a taxi before I know it. His arms are around me and he's crushing his mouth to mine. Everything else is disappearing. I want him to do more. My body melts against him when his arms tighten. I never feel so wanted, so safe, as I do when I'm in his arms. I sense his heart pounding under my hand when I slide it over his T-shirt. He's just as firm and strong as I remembered, but no memory is as good as this. The sheer bliss of his lips pressed against mine—moving, demanding, taking. And I want to give. I need to give.

His tongue slides into my mouth, and from the back of his throat comes a growl. I remember the growl. I used to hear it in my dreams. I used to wake up with a rush of raw heat between my thighs. Heat and wetness. My body starts singing a song it forgot the words to. He knows my body, he knows what I need.

We don't say a word as we hurry through the lobby of his hotel towards the elevator.

# IZZY

https://www.youtube.com/watch?v=fkLUBxLMMio
Lost on You

There is a feeling of deja-vu as we wait for the lift. I remember the feeling of his cock inside me and desperately need that again. I know I shouldn't indulge myself like this but it's all so good, so right. Nothing has ever felt so right as it does when I'm with him. I stare at the lift doors remembering our first night. I've replayed every moment of it so many times. Even last night.

Nothing has changed. Everything has been perfectly preserved.

He barely waits until the door of his room closes before grabbing me and pushing me up against it. Pressing his body to mine, he devours my mouth. With one rough movement he strips off my coat. I don't hear it fall. The blood is pounding so hard in my head.

I let my palms slide over his broad, powerful shoulders. God, I've missed him. My fingers around his neck. His hands run up and down and all over me until every nerve in my body is screaming.

Uncorking the passion I've kept bottled up since that night so long ago, I hook one leg around his and pull him in until his thigh is between mine. Fire races through me, lighting me up, reminding me how dead I've been without him, what life is really all about. I moan as I grind myself on his thigh.

"Fuck, I need you," he groans, moving from my mouth to my neck, kissing, sucking, driving me crazy. I tilt my head back and hold him close, running my fingers through his thick hair, abandoning myself to him.

It's so good. Sooo good.

His hand works on the buttons of my blouse, then pulls the material aside so he can latch onto one of my breasts through my lacy bra cup. It doesn't satisfy him and he yanks the fabric aside before sucking greedily on me again.

"Oh, God!" I cry out as I arch my back, pushing more of my breast into his mouth. He bites down on my nipple, drawing a hiss through my clenched teeth.

"Take me, Tyson, take me now," I hear myself gasp.

He cups my butt, lifting me in one swift motion. I close my legs around his waist and the pressure of his thick, hard cock against my aching pussy is sweeter than anything I could have imagined.

He lowers me gently, then crawls up the length of my body to kiss me again.

He whispers my name. It sounds heavenly from his lips. He nips the spot between my neck and my shoulder. The exact same spot he had bitten that first night when he was deep inside me. I gasp with the sensation of his mouth, his teeth, and his tongue flat against my skin. Tasting, sensing, and enjoying the fast beat of my heart in the blood that rushes through my veins.

I pull the shirt from his waistband and indulge myself in the feeling of his bare skin, marveling the way I did the first time at the size and firmness of his body. He is truly perfection. He peels his shirt off. I revel in the sight, the tattoos I've nearly forgotten, the rippling muscles, and rasp of his skin. Pulling him down for another deep, breathtaking kiss that goes on and on. I wish it would never stop. I would gladly spend the rest of my life in this moment.

"I missed you so fuckin' much," he grates hoarsely, running a hand down my side, over my hip and down the outside of my thigh. He grabs my boot, tugs it off my foot and throws it behind him. He repeats it with my other boot. I watch him unbutton my jeans and pull the zip down. Grasping the leg ends of my jeans he yanks hard, the movement so strong and sure, my jeans immediately slide down my hips, legs, and feet. He flings them away from him.

"Please ..." I moan, flexing my hips upward like an animal in heat, dying to make contact with him. I need him between my legs. I need him inside me, on top of me, pinning me to the bed with his glorious body.

He peels off my panties and looks down between my legs. Slowly, he spreads my legs and stares at my splayed open pussy as if he is starving. I feel my own wetness leak out of me as I let him look. I want him to look. The way he looks at me makes me feel beautiful, desirable, wanted. The way I haven't felt in two years.

"Look how wet you are," he says, dragging his eyes up to mine.

"It's you. You make me wet for you."

"Wrap your legs around my neck," he orders, and as I lift my legs, he throws them on either side of his shoulders. Then he dives between them. Licking a trail up my inner thigh, his beard scratching and tickling me, he moves higher and higher along the sensitive skin. His progress is maddeningly slow, and it makes me clench my hands to stop myself from grabbing his head and greedily pushing it to where I'm throbbing for his mouth.

Finally, an eternity later, he drags his tongue across my throbbing clit, and I can't help it.

I scream.

"Shhh …" he murmurs, as if he is attending to a crying baby.

Spreading my pussy lips with his fingers, he dips his tongue into me. A cry is torn out of my throat. I already know I won't last long. He laps up the juices pouring out of me, then rims my asshole.

"Tyson," I squeak.

"Not now, but I'm going in there, babe," he says with a dark laugh. Then he begins to suckle gently at my clit and my body arches off the bed. He touches parts of me that nobody's ever touched, unleashes something I didn't know existed before him. I close my eyes and let the sensations take over, abandoning myself. No more thinking. Only feeling. And there's so much to feel.

Writhing and groaning, losing control, I feel nothing but my hands clawing into his hair and his mouth on me. My ecstatic cries fill the air as my body clenches around him and waves of sheer bliss wash over me. His hands roam over me, touching, caressing, fondling, stroking.

When I come down from that dizzy height of pleasure, and my ragged breathing quiets, I hear him making growling sounds as he starts to eat me out again. Sucking my swollen, wet lips into his mouth. He's giving me more. And by God, I want more. I've been thirsting for this. I'll never get enough of him.

He barely has the condom unrolled before he's between my legs again, pulling me into a deep, searching kiss as he pushes forward. I groan, deep and low as he plunges into me. I'd forgotten how massive he is, how he filled and stretched until I thought he would split me.

"You like that?" he grunts, grinding slowly, teasing me.

After all this time, I need more. I need it to hurt. I tighten my legs around his butt and pull him deeper, grunting with the effort. More of him gets pushed in. Our bodies fit together like they were made for each other. I watch his body moving and it's like magic, his abs tightening each time he buries his cock in me.

"Go in deeper still," I gasp.

He frowns. "I don't want to hurt you."

"I want to take all of you inside me."

"Okay," he says, and pulls out of me. Sitting on his haunches, he rolls my hips so I am doubled over and both my pussy and asshole are exposed to his gaze. I lift my hips higher and look him in the eye, telling him without words that I want it harder, faster, stronger.

He opens my legs and plunges all the way in. Then, before I can even adjust to the sensation, he gives it to me the way I asked for it. Like an animal. Feral and furious. Pounding. My breasts bouncing wildly, my whole body jerking uncontrollably.

The pressure starts to build again, getting stronger every time our bodies crash together. Until I can't stand it. It's too good. He feels the change in me, the way my muscles begin to tighten around his thickness, and he pummels me faster than ever.

My orgasm rips through me and crests. I hold my arms out to him, just as the wave breaks.

"Yes. Yes," I gasp. A sob of pure joy and relief pours from my lips. My nails trace lines across his shoulders, making him groan louder as his thrusts speed up.

"Yes, I love it, harder, faster," I whisper, thrusting up to meet him, desperate to give him what he gave me. When he explodes with a roar of pleasure, my heart swells with the deep love that I have never been able to kill no matter if I thought he was an uncaring cad. I've loved him all this time.

"Hell," he groans when it's over, falling forward, pressing his mouth to my shoulder. "To think I managed to convince myself that I was imagining how fantastic it was before."

"Me, too," I whisper, kissing the side of his face, his shoulder. "Me, too."

It was so good, so right. Everything I remembered and more. We smile at each other, and just for a second the years dissolve and we're right back where we started. Intoxicated with each other. Unable to believe that we've been so lucky to find each other.

Then the real world comes back to me and dread fills my heart. I gave in to a sexual urge? It's so wrong.

It's all so wrong.

# TYSON

I stare up at the ceiling and can't help grinning like an idiot. I found her ... and drove her nuts. Two years of being without her, of longing, of regretting I never left a message at the hotel, is finally over. Two years haven't changed a thing.

The problem is, when I turn my head to face her, I don't see the same look of happiness and joy. She even seems distressed and upset. My smile goes sour before dissolving. "What is it?" I ask.

She closes her eyes for a second, then sits up. "I should go. I don't regret what we did, but it can't happen again. This ends here."

"What are you talking about?" I reach for her, brushing my fingertips over her bare back, and she jerks away like I burned her.

"Things are very different now, Tyson." I've never heard such sadness, such total hopelessness in her voice before.

I sit up, speechless, devastated. She really wants to go. Fuck if it makes sense. How could she be so passionate one minute and turn so sad the next? What's happened to her? I run my fingers through my hair and try to figure out my next move. I mucked things up once, I'm not about to do it again. If she thinks she is going to slip through my fingers so easily she's got another thing coming. "Help me to understand how it is," I say slowly.

"I'm sorry, I can't. I don't have the time. Just know that it's better for us both if I get out of here as fast as I can."

I catch her hand and tug. She falls on her back and looks up at me. "Make the time. For old times sake."

"I'm late. I've got to go. Please." I stare down at her. How could I want to fuck her again? I just did. She wriggles out of my grasp, scoots to the edge of the bed and starts looking around the room. "My purse," she mumbles. "I have to check my phone."

I point to her purse by the door, and her cheeks go pink with the memory of how she dropped it in her hurry to fuck me. Buck naked she hurries over to pick it up. There is nothing on her mind except her phone. I watch her look at the screen and the relief that crosses her face as she drops it back into her bag.

"Everything all right?" I ask casually.

"Hmm? Yeah. Thanks." She turns away and starts getting dressed. She slips into her panties, then pulls her jeans on over the top.

"Be honest with me. Why are you running away like this?" I bound out of bed. In spite of what is going on, I have a hard-on from watching her dress. She tries to avert her eyes as she looks around for her bra.

"It's much too long a story, and I don't have the time. I'm sorry, Tyson, but you'll just have to accept that."

I take her by the arm as she tries to hurry past, and I pull her to me. "I don't have to accept anything. I don't even have to let you go. I could keep you here for days, naked and with my cock inside you, and you won't be able to stop me."

"You're holding me too tight," she mutters through clenched teeth, looking at my shoulder.

I know I'm not holding her too tight. "Want me to prove it? Want me to show you how easily I could get your ass back in that bed?"

She flinches.

"Why won't you look at me, Izzy? Is it too hard to leave when you look me in the eye?"

She raises her eyes to mine. God, they're so sad. "Don't we deserve so much better than what we've had?"

She doesn't say a word—but she doesn't disagree, either, so that's something.

I capitalize on my argument. "I want us to have another chance. The chance we should've had two years ago. I swear I'm telling the truth when I say I'd have given anything for things to have gone differently, but I couldn't do a thing then. Now, it's up to us, you and me. We lost two years, but we still have the rest of our lives. We could be so happy together, Izzy. I want you. I want you in my life forever."

Tears fill her eyes. "Tyson. Don't do this. Please."

I sense her resolve waning and push in for the kill. "Don't pretend you don't feel it too. I can hear it in your voice, and see it in your eyes that you want it too. Just like you couldn't resist coming here with me today—you tried, but you couldn't do it. What's between us is too strong, Izzy. Tell me I'm wrong. Go on."

She opens her mouth, but nothing comes out except a soft sigh. Resignation. She knows I'm right, of course. The way I know I'm right.

I let go of her arm. "Izzy. Come on. Give us a chance. We could have so much. We could be so happy." I reach out for her face, stroking the soft skin of her cheek. She doesn't move. She only looks into my eyes with that same sad, longing expression. I'm offering the woman everything I have and she looks back at me like I just killed her dog.

Then her jaw tightens and she raises her chin. "I wish it were that easy. If you believe nothing else, believe that." She takes a step back from me. "Please, I need to get dressed." I watch the only woman I ever gave a damn about run around picking up and pull on the rest of her clothes. Her hands are shaking in her hurry to get out of my life. Maybe this is what I deserve. I've played fast and loose for a long time. I've broken too many hearts. I'm getting what was coming to me now. But I refuse to accept it.

"I won't give up on you. You have to know that."

"Promise me something," she mutters as she pulls on her boots.

"It depends."

him get away with it, even if I have to be especially careful for her sake.

"I don't want to be with him anymore. God, I haven't wanted to be with him for almost as long as I've been with him. He showed me his true colors early on—not early enough, sadly. What a stupid fool I was to fall for his fake charm and empty promises."

"You did what you thought was right." I think of him as a vulture circling an empty sky, waiting, heartless. An innocent girl like her—so beautiful, so precious and untainted. He must've thought he hit the jackpot, the monster.

"I do want to be with you." She kisses my cheek, my jaw, my mouth. "I do, I do. It's so unfair. Why did life have to turn out this way?"

She's killing me. She's twisting the knife in my heart and making it all but impossible not to march out of the hotel and track Tony Jackson down and snap his neck. I kiss her back, tasting the salty tears. "I know," I whisper, stroking her hair, her back. "I know. It isn't fair."

She touches her forehead to mine. "Maybe there's a way to protect my family before I leave him. I've been thinking about it. I think it's possible if I play it safe. He might be leaving town tonight for a few days—if I can do it then ..."

She's so desperate. So painfully desperate. I want to wrap her in my arms and never let her go. Just let that bastard try to get to her while I'm holding her. Then again, it isn't just her. It's her family. Even so, I would move heaven and earth for her. She needs only give me the word. "Don't do anything yet. I'll be here for you. Whatever you want, we'll make it happen. Let me think about this. Let me come up with a good plan for us and your family. Don't take any chances tonight," I warn her anxiously.

She laughs humorlessly. "Trust me, I won't."

"Are you able to come here tomorrow at noon. I'll have a plan by then."

"All right. I'll meet you here. Noon tomorrow."

"How are you going to get back?" I ask.

"I'll just take a taxi."

She finishes getting her things together and I hold her tight before she dashes out the door. I've become paranoid so I feel as if it's the last time I'll ever touch her.

"Wait! Wait!" I catch her before she gets on the elevator.

"What is it?"

"Let's exchange numbers this time. Let's not make the same mistake."

She shakes her head. "No. Don't ever call me. Even if I delete a number he has a contact at the phone company and gets a list of all the numbers that I call or call me."

"What?" I explode.

She touches my face. "It's okay. It's just something he does. Tell me your number. I will remember it and call you from the phone box just outside my apartment complex if anything happens or I can't make it. Otherwise I'll meet you here tomorrow.

I give her my number and make her repeat it numerous times.

I swallow the overpowering urge not to let her go back to him. It makes my hands clench. "Call me if anything changes. All right?" She nods before hurrying away.

# IZZY

It might be possible. It just might. My heart is soaring with hope. I can't remember the last time I thought anything good was possible for me anymore. It's been so long. I felt like an old woman, like my life might as well be over at the age of twenty-four. Like nothing good would ever happen again. He makes me believe that there's a chance, after all. If we could find each other again, who knows what else is possible?

I'm actually smiling as I walk through the door to my apartment. Not my choice of a place to live, but then I've not had many choices in the last couple of years. It's either comply or face the painful consequences.

"Where've you been?"

I freeze instantly at the sound of his voice. Shit! He's got to be the devil, he absolutely must be, or else I would've heard him breathing or felt his presence. Something. Instead, he's tricked me into thinking I was secure. He's always tricking me.

lost. Were it not for my mom and Christopher I would have walked out the first day he laid a hand on me.

I stare at a blank wall.

I already know what will happen tonight. He will come around and want me to have sex with him. While fucking me he will keep banging into my bruises. He'll pretend they are accidents, but I know he does it deliberately. Then when he comes he will choke me again.

I spend the day huddled up in the apartment, licking my wounds, and drinking enough tea to make me feel waterlogged and sluggish. Charlotte calls.

"I need to talk to you," I say.

"What about?" she asks warily.

"Tell you when I see you."

She makes a sound of despair. "He's hurt you again, hasn't he?"

"No, no," I lie. "It's not about that. It's about that cake recipe I asked you about." Cake recipe is our code word for fake passports.

There is a pause. "Oh, that," she says super casually. "Of course. I will look for it tonight. When do you want to meet?"

"In a couple of days."

"Damn that stupid wanker. You need a couple of days to recover, don't you?" she demands furiously.

"I've got to go, babe, but I'll talk to you tomorrow, okay?" I end the call and wander to the kitchen. A look in the fridge only depresses me. I have next to nothing. Yesterday was food shopping day, but because I met Tyson, I didn't go to the supermarket.

There's enough in my purse for bread, milk, and a few other things, so I bundle up and put on my sunglasses even though it's well past sunset. Everybody knows what a woman wearing dark glasses at night is trying to hide, but it's better to have someone shake their head and click their tongue than to let anyone actually see how hideous I look. When I was younger I thought of women who stay with men who abuse them as pathetic. Now I am one of them.

It is with that shame I walk through the door of the corner shop. Mr. Rama's wife always comes in the evening to spend a bit of time with her husband so she is also behind the counter. They are a sweet couple who call out to me cheerfully.

As they bag up my things they talk to me about the weather and are kind enough to pretend not to acknowledge the elephant in the room. Sometimes I fantasize about telling other people. Telling anybody who could help me.

Yes, he hits me. Hard. Yes, I'm bruised. Frequently. No, I don't like it. Yes, I'm desperate to leave him, but I can't. He'll kill me. Worse, he'll kill my son. He'll probably kill my son while I watch, just for spite. That's what a monster he is, that's how sick he is. But all of this goes unsaid as I thank them for their help and pick up my bag.

The moment I turn the corner to walk down the quiet path leading to my apartment block, a tall figure steps in front of me. I'm so skittish and nervous I jump back with a cry of fear, ready to run.

"Wait, wait! It's just me. Just me." Tyson takes my arms and I flinch, wincing with pain. His jaw drops. "Jesus Christ. Sunglasses."

"How did you find me?" I gasp.

His eyes search my face anxiously. "I had a private investigator trace your phone call and I came here immediately and waited for you. I knew you'd have to get out of your apartment complex at some time."

I look around, panic stricken. "You have to get out of here. Now."

"What's with the glasses?" he whispers. "It's fucking dark, Izzy."

"I have an eye infection," I rattle off. One of my many excuses. It usually works. Not this time.

"I just saw you yesterday and your eyes were fine. Try again."

"Please, leave me alone. I have to get back before somebody sees us." I try to move back, but in a flash he has grasped my hand. He reaches out and takes off the sunglasses. His face goes blank for a moment before his eyes narrow to slits and the area around his mouth goes white.

"I'll fucking kill him," he spits. "So help me God, Izzy, I'll kill that bastard for what he's done to you!"

"You'll get me killed standing out here talking to me, saying things like this!" I hiss. I can barely think for terror. If Tony were to show up right now … I whip my head around, but the street behind us is virtually empty. Thank God for that.

"I'll kill him. I'll kill him with my bare hands, Izzy. I'll take pleasure in it, I swear," Tyson snarls.

"Yes, and I would love to see it," I blurt out. Suddenly, I feel tired. So damned tired. If only I could unburden this terrible weight on someone else. Just for a moment. My shoulders sag and I exhale.

"Let me help you, Izzy," Tyson says softly.

The temptation to say yes, help me, is so strong I have to bite my tongue.

"Come on Izzy. You can't go back to him. I'll take you somewhere safe right now."

"There is nowhere safe you can take me. Why don't I meet you tomorrow and we can talk then? He is coming to see me tonight."

I have never seen any man look the way he did when I said he is coming tonight. It was murderous rage.

"You know nothing about me if you think I am going to let that sick pervert anywhere near you again."

I look at him in a panic. "You don't understand. I can't just leave."

He looms above me, his hands clenched tight at his sides. "Why not?"

I think fast. This is getting dangerous. His hotel is not too far from here, and I need to tell him about Christopher, anyway. If anything were to happen to me, he needs to know he has a son. Yesterday taught me how fragile my situation is. I should have told him the truth, the full truth yesterday, but I thought I could keep him from entangling with Tony. Christopher needs to know his father if I die or otherwise disappear …

"Come on. Let's get you dressed. We have to act quickly."

"Where is Christopher now?" he asks, zipping up my dress.

"With my mother. He doesn't live with me. It is too dangerous"

He nods. "All right. Where is Tony? Right now?"

"I—I don't know ..."

"You said he was going out of town, right?"

"He told me he was going to, but yesterday he said he didn't have to anymore. To be honest, I don't know. He might have been trying to trick me. I've had to second-guess everything he's ever told me."

He nods. "You'll never have to see him again, and he will never hurt my son."

I wish his words were a comfort. I wish I could collapse in his arms and believe that everything will be all right. Instead, all I can do is sob softly because I know it is not going to be that easy.

# TYSON

"Are you sure we shouldn't wait for a bit?" Izzy's eyes are wide with fear as we go down to the hotel basement where my car is parked. I know I'm not in a position to get her level of fear, but I'm going to do everything I can to help her understand I don't fear him at all and he can no longer hurt her. Ever.

"Yes, I'm sure," I say gently. "We can't wait another second to do this." Unlocking my door, I help her inside. She winces as she leans back. Fuck, I can't even think about what he did without wanting to beat the shit out of him. Let's see what a big hero he is when he has to deal with someone his own size.

My head is buzzing as I follow her directions to her mother's house. My Izzy is with a man who beats her. I have a boy. A son.

She looks around nervously when I park in front of a block of apartments. Other than a few teenagers playing with their bikes there is no one around. We get out and walk to her door. She puts her key through the door and before she can push it open, a woman who looks like an older version of her is standing in the hallway. Her face is white and she looks terrified. At the sight of her daughter her hand clasps her chest.

"I don't know what I thought when I heard your key," she mumbles. "I knew you wouldn't be coming here at this time. I thought ... oh God ..."

"It's okay, Mom. Everything is okay. This is Christopher's dad, Tyson."

"Hello, Ma'am," I greet with a polite nod.

Her eyes skitter to me then back to her daughter.

"He's going to help us. We don't have much time though. We have to hurry and get out of here," Izzy says.

Her mother's eyes widen, but she doesn't ask any questions. Just nods her agreement. Almost as if she was waiting for this moment. Hoping somebody would come along and save her daughter.

"Only take whatever you need for tonight. We can buy everything else tomorrow," I say.

"I'll get Christopher and his stuff. You go get yours, Mom. Just pack a small bag."

Silently, Izzy's mother turns to obey her daughter.

"Please leave any mobile phones or laptops behind," I instruct.

Her mother nods and scuttles away. Izzy takes my hand and we go upstairs. She opens a door and steps into a blue room illuminated by a night light by a cot. My feet won't move. I stand stock still at the threshold. All my life I wanted my own family. Brothers, sisters, a father, and I never had it. Even the sad, alcoholic mother I had was taken away from me, but in this little blue room is my family. All mine. Made from my own seed.

Izzy turns back to look at me, her eyes questioning, curious. "What is it?"

"Nothing," I say softly, but I'm so choked with emotion I can barely get the word out.

She tugs at my hand again, and suddenly I can't get to the cot fast enough. I follow her eagerly. A child is sleeping, his fat arm thrown over his face. I stare transfixed. Gently, she moves his arm away and I see his face. He is, without doubt, the most beautiful thing I have ever seen.

My son. This is my son. I think of my mother. How she would have loved to have seen him. Something unfurls inside me. Love for him fills my heart until it feels as if my heart will burst. I will die for this tiny life. To think of Tony threatening this innocent angel makes my blood boil.

"Oh, Izzy. I can't believe I missed everything," I whisper. My voice sounds broken.

"You won't miss anything, anymore," she says softly.

"Never again," I promise.

She puts her hands into the cot and lifts up our sleeping child. It must have hurt her, because she winces slightly as she adjusts him against her body. Turning to me, she says, "Do you want to hold him?"

I swallow hard. "Won't I wake him up?"

"It will take an earthquake to wake him up," she says with a smile.

I don't smile back. I can't. I'm too happy. Too proud. Too amazed. "Are you sure about this? I've never carried a baby."

"See how I've got him. Fold your arms in the same way, and I'll just put him in that cradle like space."

I copy the position of her arms and she lay Christopher into them. Maybe it comes from working with horses, but as soon as she puts my son into my arms, my body instantly loses its anxiety that I wouldn't be able to do it properly, that I'll drop or hurt him. He is so tiny my hand can support his whole head. My hands go around Christopher naturally, protectively. I lift our child up to my face and kiss his soft cheek tenderly. He smells of milk and innocence.

I look at Izzy's face and she is nodding. Her eyes are full of joyful tears as if she just saw the proof she needed that she made the right decision to trust me. The heavy burden of protecting Christopher from Tony all on her own has been magically lifted from her shoulders. As if the sight of me with Christopher in my arms is everything she has ever dreamed for the last two years.

For an eternity we stare at each other, both of us lost in our own joy and the little being we created. Then her phone rings and she jumps like a startled cat. She takes her phone out of her bag, looks at it, and back up to me.

"It's him," she whispers.

"Don't answer it. Get Christopher's things. Quickly."

She runs around the room throwing essentials into a yellow overnight bag. In minutes she is ready. We go out of the room and she knocks one of the other doors on that floor.

"Are you ready, Mom?" I hear her ask.

"Yes," her mother replies coming out.

We go down the stairs and out into the night. The teenagers are still there with their bikes. I curse, but there is no way around it. They turn to look at us. No wonder. We make an unusual sight. We look like we are running away.

I settle my son in his grandmother's lap at the back and carefully put Izzy in the front passenger seat. I am worried that she might have broken ribs. I need to get her to a doctor in the morning.

"Where are we going?" Izzy asks as we drive away.

"You'll find out when we get there. You wouldn't know where we are going even if I told you," I explain, glancing into the rearview mirror to make sure we are not being followed. Tony's not the only one with connections. I'm taking them to a gypsy camp.

It will be a shock to Izzy and her mother, but I trust these people implicitly. I have to take my family where even the cops will not dare to tread. It's too dangerous for them, but not dangerous for me or my family.

Our surroundings start to get a bit dodgy after thirty minutes of driving out of London. We don't talk much. Finally, we turn off the motorway into Hounslow. I take a dirt road to a gypsy caravan site. Even though it is already dark, children run towards our car.

"Are you sure this is a good idea?" Izzy's mother asks anxiously as she sees the caravans.

"It's the best shot we have," I murmur as I steer the car over the narrow path.

"Tony, his men or the cops will not dare come here. There is no one here who will betray us. These people are fiercely loyal and protective of their own kind," I explain as I navigate the car between two stone walls connecting the east and west side of the camp. There aren't many lights on in the windows, but I still see faces peering out at us. The ladies must see them, too. A look in the rearview mirror shows a very worried looking woman.

"It's not the Ritz, but it's temporary and it's the safest place for the three of you," I say.

"Won't you be staying with us?" Izzy asks worriedly.

"No. I need a bit of time to arrange things for us."

"We'll be fine here, Tyson. You go on ahead and do what needs to be done," Izzy's mother says firmly.

I catch her gaze in the mirror. "Thank you. I promise there is no safer place you can be. I've spent more time here than I care to recall," I say as I park the car between a ditch and a pile of rubbish. It doesn't do much to settle their minds, I'm sure. I turn to them. "As a boy, I had a lot of friends in this village. I know it like the back of my hand, and the people here know me."

"You're friends with gypsies?" Izzy asks, looking around us with a dazed expression.

"Yes. I know. Crazy, right? Rich boy is friends with gypsies.

I'm actually half-gypsy. After I ran away from the correction center I lived with them for many years. I wanted to run free, and that is what I did with them. It's where my love of horses comes from. I know the woman who lives in that house," I say pointing to the one on my left. "Mariella is a truly terrible cook, but she is a good woman."

"What if Tony does track us here?" Izzy asks.

"Then God help him. Those people are lovely and very welcoming. They would give you the shirt off their back, all of them, but they'll also show Tony he's not half as tough as he thinks he is if he tries to start trouble. Believe me. I've seen them handle themselves."

Mother and daughter look at each other, having a silent conversation.

I add, "It won't be forever. Just until I can think of something more permanent. My top priority at the moment is keeping all of you someplace where he can't find you. I need to be able to make my plans without having to worry about what he'll do to you."

"No," Izzy whispers, turning to me. "Now, I'll have to worry about what he's going to do to you."

"He doesn't even know I exist ... yet. But he will."

"I hope you're right."

"I can take care of myself, Izzy. You just stay safe here."

Mariella opens the door before we can even reach it. She comes out with her arms open and envelops me in a warm, soft hug. "Oh, my boy. It's so good to see you again."

"Thank you for doing this," I say close to her ear.

She pulls away from me and looks at me incredulously. "After everything you did for me and my boys? This is nothing."

I introduce my family to her and she grins widely. "I've made a lovely dinner for everybody." I look at Izzy, and for the first time since she called yesterday to say she won't be turning up, I smile.

She widens her eyes. "You are staying for dinner, aren't you?"

I pat my stomach. "Would love to, but I just had food. Couldn't manage a thing."

Izzy grins back. She looks happy.

I wait long enough for them to get settled in before I say my goodbyes. Izzy touches my arm. "Please. Come back and collect us quickly," she whispers. "Not because I don't like being here or anything, but I do hate being without you."

I pull her close to me and inhale her scent with my entire being. She makes me feel like a king, like I could do anything. All I want to do right now is to start our life together, but I'll have to be patient. I've waited this long. I can wait a few more days.

"I'll come back soon. I promise." I kiss her gently on the side of her swollen lip, and run the back of my fingers on her cheek. I have said goodbye too many times to this girl. If I am smart and play my cards right this could be the last time.

# TYSON

Ralph did offer to stay and take care of the farm, but I told him to go to his big family gathering five miles away. It'll be good for me to go back to the farm. My best thinking time is early in the morning when I am astride one of my horses and galloping across the open fields. I feel good that I have taken Izzy and Christopher away from Tony.

By now he would know they are gone. My family are safe for the time being, but I need a plan quickly. One doesn't rest on their laurels when they're dealing with a psychopath.

I know my enemy. I've done my research. He's a nasty, vile, disgusting excuse for a human being who is already linked to at least a half-dozen murders. Those I know about are only the ones the police are actually aware of. There might be dozens of others. People who didn't know when to leave well enough alone, who tried to testify against him in court, or who wouldn't back down when he threatened them.

Izzy's face floats in the front of my mind's eye. Beautiful, fragile, injured. He'll never hurt her again, not as long as there's breath left in my body. I think of my son with wonder. I don't think I've fully appreciated him yet. Even the thought is amazing. My mind drifts to the future. I can already see myself teaching him to ride. Giving him a real childhood in the country with horses, and dirt, and values. It'll be a sweet life.

I'll make it a sweet life.

The first step of my plan has to be drawing up a will and making Izzy completely self-sufficient should anything happen to me. I immediately call my lawyer's office and leave a message for him to call me in the morning.

I only stopped once to get some sandwiches, but by the time I get back to Suffolk it is after midnight. I open the front door and I'm in such a hurry to start work I don't even bother to switch on any lights or switch on the heating. I go straight to the back of the house where my office is. As I'm firing up my laptop I hear gravel in the driveway crunching. A car is coming from the direction of the stables and halting in front of the house.

For a second I freeze. I'm not expecting anybody. I'm in the country and never in the whole time I have lived here has anybody visited at this time of the night. As impossible as it seems it has to be Tony's men. How could he have found me so quickly? Then I remember the teenagers. The way they watched us. It would be so easy for a man who has access to law enforcement databases to trace my car. When I hear car doors shut quietly, I snap out of my disbelief. There is more than one of them. Three. My hand moves towards the switch on my desk table. I snap it off.

Then, I'm out of my chair and streaking across the room. I

grab the bat that usually lies collecting dust on the counter and go out to the living room. Not making a sound, I move towards the doorway.

I hear their voices. They're already outside the front door. I position myself to the right of the door when I hear a rough voice say, "Just kick the fucking door in already!"

"Forget that door. It's solid. Come around here," another voice says closer to the French doors at the side of the house. In a flash, I run over to the French doors.

Bang!

The door flies open. I raise the bat over my shoulder and wait. As one of the men passes through I swing it as hard as I can at head height. The sound of wood cracking against a skull echoes through the high-ceilinged entryway. A brutish looking thug drops like a sack of potatoes in the open doorway.

"What the fuck?" Two other men stumble over the body but manage to stay on their feet. They don't know yet, but they're in trouble—deep trouble. One of them holds a knife and the other holds a machete. In a split second my brain has made a note of the fact that the knife and machete are dripping with blood.

Whose blood?

I need to get them before they get me. Instinct and the desire to survive take over. The machete is my biggest threat, so I turn to him first.

His crooked smile widens as he raises his arms, and the moonlight filtering in through the open doorway glints off the metal. He is a big guy. Strong, but clumsy. Instead of trying to attack his arms, I go low. A good blow across his kneecaps makes him howl in pain. I'm fairly sure I heard a bone shatter. At least one of his knees crushed from the blow.

"Fuck! You fucking broke my knees," he screams, curling into a ball.

Now the knife and the gorilla holding it. He glances at his mate, then back at me. There is fear in his eyes. He hadn't expected me to be so effective with just a bat. With a roar he lunges at me with the knife pointed at my stomach. A quick sidestep and a back kick knocks him off-balance. He mutters a curse before I whip a brisk blow straight to his balls.

He bellows, his eyes bulging, but no sound comes out of his mouth. I watch the veins of his neck pop as he drops like a stone. The knife skitters across the floor as he cups his privates, shrieking silently in agony while his friend with the busted knee is screaming abuse at me.

I make quick work of kicking their weapons out of their reach. Better to be safe than sorry. The car sitting outside is a Range Rover. I go out and have a look—the keys are still in the ignition for a fast getaway. I start the engine, then go back in the house.

"Come on you lot," I grunt, dragging them one by one to the car.

They're in too much pain to fight me as I push them inside—the one I hit across the side of the head is still totally out of it. I throw him across the back seat and slam the door shut.

The other two look like they're in such pain, they'd rather be dead. I can only imagine, especially the one whose balls I turned to jelly. He deserved a lot worse than that, coming at me with a knife. I lean on the car and tap the driver's window until Jelly Balls rolls it down. "Make no mistake," I snarl, glaring at them. "If you come back here, I'll kill you next time. Tell Tony he got off easy."

Mr. Broken Kneecaps looks up at me, his face twisted with pain. "I wouldn't be so smug if I were you. You have no idea what you are dealing with. Tony will never stop until you return his woman."

"He'll burn in hell before that happens," I growl.

The car speeds off, tires crunching over the gravel. When they are about twenty yards he hangs his head out of the window and shouts, "Left a surprise for you at the stables."

# TYSON

https://www.youtube.com/watch?v=NrIL-0AtDY4
Now we are free

A cold wind blows as I turn my head towards the stables, five hundred yards away. The stable doors are open. Oh God!

The blood on the machete!

I start running. Running so hard I feel the rush of wind bite into my face. I stand at the threshold of the stables panting hard. I can already smell the fear and sweet smell of blood. I step into it. In disbelief. This cannot be happening. No way. Even as I turn my head to look in the first stall I refuse to believe it. Not animals. Not such beautiful, blameless animals.

Rubina lies dead in the first stall.

"No, no, no," I mutter, running to the next stall. Jenny's blood is slowly collecting in a thick pool of dark liquid under her head.

I turn to the next stall, horrified, unable to think, speak, rationalize.

Who would do this?

The monsters.

The unspeakable monsters!

Khan lies on his side. His eyes are open and his breath is labored, but he is not dead. His neck has been ripped open, the flesh raw and pink. He looks at me with his big shocked eyes. I rush to him and fall to my haunches. I cup my palms on either side of his face. My whole body is shaking with fury.

He makes a grunting sound of terrible pain.

"Shhhh … It's okay. It's okay. I'm here now," I say as I twist my hand hard. I hear his neck breaking. The life goes out of my friend instantly. His eyes stare vacantly. There is no more pain.

I stand up and walk to the next stall. Matilda, whom I have loved for the last eight years is dead. With my bare hands I break Riley's neck. Then I go to Fey's stall. I kept her for last because I didn't want to see the destruction. Fey was pregnant. She was due to foal any day now. I take a deep breath and turn the corner.

Fey is lying very still on her side in a pool of blood, but a single straw next to her nose is moving gently. I rush to her side and drop to my knees next to her. Her eyes are glazed with shock. There is no recognition in them. She is almost gone. I kiss her face and whisper in her ear, "I love you. Hang on, I'll save the little un for you."

I run back to the house. Panting hard, I go to the kitchen and pull out the sharp meat knife from the wooden block. I grab rags from the cupboard. Then I sprint back to Fey's stall.

"You did very well, Fey. Very well. I'm so proud of you," I whisper before I break her neck.

As soon as I hear the crack I place the knife at the top of her belly and I slice her all the way down her underside. Hot blood pours out over my hands. I reach into her steaming organs and pull her womb out. I cut the sac and free the baby. I pull it out and it lies on the ground pale and still. Refusing to come to this cruel earth that took its mother away before it was even born.

Gently, I massage its limbs. "Come on, baby. Come on," I plead to the tiny thing.

God knows how long I gently massage it, but finally I have to give up. I throw my head back and roar with fury. I look down at the still animal and I know rage like I have never known in my life. It is like a ball of fire in my belly. I will hunt every one of those men and I will rip their hearts out of their chests. They don't deserve to live. They killed my horses. These blameless beautiful animals. I stand up and turn away.

As I take the first step I hear a slight rustling sound.

For a fraction of a second I freeze with astonishment. Then I turn around and look at the little foal. Its head is moving. It is trying to breathe! I drop down on my hands and knees and scoop it into my arms. I take it away to the place where it should have been born. There is fresh straw laid out there. It will be away from the stench of fear and blood. The first thing it sees will not be the gruesome sight of its mother with her guts ripped out of her. It will be me.

It's mother, it's father, it's protector.

I lay it down gently and wait for it to slowly raise its head. Unsteadily, it does and tears start pouring out of my eyes. I remember once being angry with my father for destroying my mother's life. If he had not left her she wouldn't have become the sad drunk she was.

She laid her hands on my cheeks and said, "There is beauty even in ashes. Out of the ashes you came."

"Welcome to the world, Phoenix," I whisper brokenly.

# TYSON

When he is able to stand, I bundle him up and put him into the horse transporter. I drive him to a friend of mine three hours away. He is experienced and has a mare that has just foaled and she might allow Phoenix to nurse from her. By the time I drop Phoenix off with my friend it is already four in the morning. I get back on the road almost immediately and call Ralph.

He is an early riser and picks up on the third ring. I try to tell him what happened to the horses without breaking down. His horror and shock is so deep I don't think his faith in human beings will ever return again. I inform him I have business to take care of in London and he tells me not to worry, he'll take care of everything at the farm.

Ralph is not a violent man, but as he hangs up he says, "Make those fuckers pay." He ends the call without saying goodbye.

It is not fully light when I get to the cemetery. The air is very still as I walk down the path to my mother's grave. It is clear to me now. Things have already gotten out of hand. He wants war. He's got one.

I lay the flowers I bought at the petrol station on Mom's grave and sit next to it. There is no one around. The sky is just beginning to lighten.

"Mom, I know I promised I'd never tell anyone that Dad is my father, but I have to break that promise. I wouldn't do it for me. You know that. I never once let on when I was in all those foster homes. I never told anyone ever, but your grandson is in danger now. If I don't do something then they'll kill him, Mom. I'm sorry. If not for him I would have taken your secret to the grave. I hope you forgive me, Mom."

I feel my throat choke up. I close my eyes and suddenly I can see my mother. I was only four or five. It was before she started drinking heavily. We found a butterfly trapped in our house. We ran around opening all the doors and windows to let it escape. Finally, it found a window and flew out. She looked at me and smiled. "We saved it, Ty. We saved him."

I feel a light brush on my arm and my eyes snap open. A yellow butterfly has landed on my skin. I stare at it, shocked as it flaps his wings a few times.

"Hello,' I whisper.

And suddenly a feeling a peace envelops me. I feel good. A gentle breeze blows in my face. The butterfly flaps its wings again. I lift my hand, but the butterfly does not fly away. I bring it close to my face and look at it. I am so close I can make out its big shiny eyes. For a while neither of us moves.

The words appear in my head. "There is nothing to forgive."

As soon as the thought comes into my head the butterfly

flaps its wings and floats away. I watch it until it flies out of sight. Then I stand up and walk away.

There is nothing to forgive. Everything was over when my mother breathed her last breath. There is no more obligation. It was something I swore I would never do, not under any circumstance, but that was before other lives were involved. Now I must do what is right for Izzy and my son.

I'll go see my half-brother Jake. I never forgot the tall boy from all those years ago. There was something commanding about him even then. Even though I never wanted to have anything to do with any of them, or even be reminded they existed, I've never been able to stop myself from reading about Jake Eden. The article claimed that he took over from one of the biggest gangland leaders in North of London. The article was based on pure speculation and anecdotes from anonymous sources since there was no evidence either way, but the author of the article seemed certain that Jake Eden was the famous Crystal Jake.

Once I even saw him. I walked into a club and there he was. He didn't see me. I stood in the shadows and watched him. He was with three other men. One of the men I recognized. He was the leader of a Russian Mafia gang. The four of them were sitting at a table in a corner speaking as equals.

Once Jake turned his head in my direction, and I saw that he was no longer the smiling boy of years back. He had cold eyes. I knew then the article was right. He had taken over. He had become the leader of one of the most brutal gangs in London.

# JAKE EDEN

I pick up a paper at reception, get into the lift, and hit the button for my floor. When the doors open I stroll into my secretary, Eliza's, office. She looks at me strangely.

"Your brother is here," she says.

I don't break my stride. "Dom or Shane?"

"Neither?"

I turn to her. "What?"

She raises her eyebrows. "He says he's your brother."

I look at her with a bemused expression. Is she serious? "I only have two brothers."

"Apparently, his name is Tyson Eden."

"What?"

"He claims he's your half-brother."

I shake my head in wonder. The world is so full of scammers, and some of them are bolshy enough to try and take me on. "Did he show proof of identity?"

"Nope."

I frown. "Where is he now?"

"In your office."

My eyebrows rise in surprise. "You let a complete stranger into my office? One that didn't even bother to identify himself?"

She nods, a funny expression on her face. "Yeah."

What the fuck is going on? I stride to my door, open it and come to a dead stop. No wonder Eliza let him decide where he should wait. The cocky bastard is sitting in my chair with his ankles crossed, and up on my table. Even in weather cold enough to freeze your bollocks off, he is wearing the gypsy uniform, a string vest. His chest and arms are covered in tattoos. His face … it's like looking into a fucking mirror.

*Dad, you old dog, you!*

I lean against the side of the door. "You're sitting in my chair."

He doesn't smile. "Looks like it, doesn't it?"

"Also looks like you didn't just discover you're my half-brother."

He nods. "True. I remember clearly cursing you and my father and your entire family my whole life."

"Care to enlighten me as to why?"

He shrugs. "Your father impregnated my mother and left her without any money or support."

"He was not the most responsible father."

He looks like he wants to vomit. "I waited outside your house once. I saw him playing happy families with you and your brother."

I frown. "When did you know about us?"

"When I was six."

I stare at him curiously. "Why the return now?"

"I need help."

I chuckle. I'm beginning to like this kid. "See, if I needed help from a man, I wouldn't go putting my feet on his desk."

"No, you wouldn't. You'd just burn his whole building down."

I'm impressed. He's done his homework. "That's more my brother's style, but I guess I have been known to do that too."

He drops his feet to the ground and comes towards me. He is the same height as Shane, but with Dom's build. Dad's build. He stands in front of me. There are fine wrinkles around his eyes. Those you get from squinting in the sun. He looks me in the eye and instantly I know that we will become good friends one day. Underneath the cocky attitude is a man with a heavy burden.

"Will you help me?" he asks.

I smile. "It's always dangerous to agree to help someone when you have no idea what they want help with, but yes. We are blood brothers. Of course, I'll do everything in my power for you. Come sit down and tell me what you need done."

I close the door, and start walking towards my bar. "Can I get you anything to drink? Coffee? Whiskey?"

"Whiskey," he says, dropping into one of the chairs in front of my desk.

I grab the crystal decanter and pour us both a double even though it is only eight in the morning. I hold his drink out to him, and he takes it from me. His hands are calloused. He is a man who works with his hands. I walk around the desk and sink into my leather chair. It is still warm from his body. What a turn up for the books.

Momentarily, I think of my poor mother. Even from the grave my father reaches out and hurts her. I'll think about it later when I have solved the problem in front of me. I buzz Eliza and tell her to hold all my calls.

Then I lean back in my chair and gaze into the face that is so similar to mine. We look so much alike it's uncanny—except his skin is more sun-kissed, and his eyes are full of goodness. He has not lived the life I have. "So …"

"To start with I have to say that I'm dealing with an enemy who might be even more ruthless than you," he says.

"I doubt it." I chuckle softly. Relief flits across his face. Poor guy. He's cut up about something. Must involve a girl.

"To cut a long story short, Tony Jackson is after me because he believes I have taken his girl although the truth is I met her first. A strange twist of fate separated us and we only saw each other again two days ago."

My eyebrows fly up to my hairline. Well, well, I certainly didn't see that coming. "You've taken Tony Jackson's woman."

"She's not his woman," he growls, eyes flashing. "She's mine. He was forcing her to be with him. She doesn't want him. She's in love with me. Also, she is the mother of my son."

I rub my face thoughtfully. Tony Jackson is an ass. He is neither strong nor powerful. Without his father he would have been put away a long time ago. His crew is vicious though. I take a swig of my drink. Whoa, it's been a long time since I drank so early in the morning. "How about you start by telling me the long version?"

I listen to him tell me about his Izzy and how they met. I see his eyes soften as he talks about her. His sadness from losing his best friend and how he lost track of her as a result. Finding her again, finding out about his son, and knowing the man she was involved with was a gangster protected by a judge.

"Where is your family now?" I ask.

"I've hidden them away in Hounslow in a gypsy camp."

I smile. "Smart move. I would have done the same."

He leans in, his hands spread on the desk. "I knew Tony would never dare set foot in the village when he knows it's your territory. Even if Tony knows where they are, he won't dare set foot in your territory. However, he knows where I live now, and he's already sent three goons to take care of me."

"But you took care of them, I'm guessing, judging from how healthy you look," I murmur.

"Yeah, well, I picked up a few tricks from my misspent youth." His jaw clenches. "I couldn't save my horses, though. The bastards slaughtered them before I got there."

"They killed your horses?" I don't know why I'm surprised, that is exactly the kind of lowdown thing Tony's men would do.

"They killed my horses," he confirms flatly. There is no emotion in his voice, but a muscle is ticking hard in his jaw. I know that look. It only means one thing: he's hurting for revenge.

"And you want me to take him for you?" I ask softly.

"No, I'll do the dirty work myself. I want you to make sure that Izzy and Christopher are safe if anything happens to me. If I don't make it."

# TYSON

J ake stares at me. "Have you killed a man before?"

"No," I say abruptly.

He nods. "I have and let me tell you, when you kill a man you are forever linked to him. You can never wash away the taint of his soul on yours. You'll never sleep the way you slept before you took another's life."

"I see no other way. I know Izzy and my son will never be safe while he is alive. I don't want to live the rest of my life constantly watching my back. If Izzy is late back from the supermarket or the hairdresser, I don't want to immediately start worrying that he has abducted her."

He fixes his cold eyes on me. "Here's some free advice for you, Tyson. Never go looking for ashes. Let the wind bring them to you."

"What do you mean?"

I think of Phoenix. Of my mother's words. "If I gave you another way out, would you take it?"

I don't have to think. "I'll do anything that would keep Izzy safe."

He smiles slowly. "Good. I know the good Judge Jackson. Very well. Much better than he realizes, in fact."

"I'm listening."

"The judge as a few hair curling secrets he wouldn't like made public. He's a nasty little fucker when he wants to be." He picks up the phone and dials without explaining what he's doing.

"Hey, John. Yup. Sure. Need to ask you a favor. Judge Jackson." Jake winks at me. "Mm-hmm. He comes to see one of your girls, doesn't he? When's he next in? Sure. I'll wait." He pauses. "Lunch break tomorrow. Who does he see? Evanna? What is she? Ah, a humiliatrix? Perfect. Right. Tell her to turn it on, no-stops, go all the way, balls to the wall. Literally. I'll need the video."

"What the hell was all that about?" I ask when he hangs up.

"Watch and see, little brother. Watch and see."

"Okay. What next?"

"Next you meet the rest of your family."

I rear back, surprised. "You want me to be part of your family?"

"Don't you think it is time?"

"I don't know. I hated you guys for such a long time."

He shrugs dismissively. "You were a child. You didn't know better. My home is the safest place for you."

"I still have to go and see Izzy."

He frowns. "No. I'll send someone to look in on her. You do not leave my sight until this is sorted out. Tony is a fool and he doesn't know his boundaries so he could be accidentally dangerous. Who have you left Izzy with?"

"Mariella."

"Right." He picks up the phone and tells someone to go and keep an eye on Mariella's house. Then he calls someone else and tells him he has family with Mariella, can they round up the boys and make sure no one gets anywhere near Mariella's house?

He stands and starts walking towards the door. "You can call Mariella's house from here. I presume you have her number. I'll be waiting outside."

I pick up the phone and call Izzy.

'Hey, how are you?"

"I'm fine, but I miss you so much, Tyson. So much."

"Me too. It won't be long. How's the little tiger?"

"Let me put him on."

I hear her go get the child and put the receiver to his ear.

"Hello," I say, my heart in my mouth. I'm talking to my son.

"Da. Da," he says, and I nearly sob for joy. It is the sweetest sound I've heard. My son recognizes me.

Izzy comes back on the phone. "That's the only word he knows."

"He's beautiful, Izzy. You did an amazing job."

Her voice drops to a whisper. "Do you know what I had for dinner last night?"

I laugh. "What?"

"Bacon and cabbage, but I have never tasted anything so vile in my life and Mom says neither has she. We ate it out of gratitude because she was so nice and so happy to have us we didn't want to hurt her, but it gave Mom a bad stomach all night. Mom made breakfast, I'm cooking tonight."

I grip the phone hard because I have to fight the urge not to get into my car and go see her. "How are your bruises?"

"They're fine. I've had worse."

"What if your ribs are broken?"

"Nah, I know what that feels like and this pain is not the same."

I breathe out slowly. Jake is right. Let the wind bring the ashes to you. Don't go looking for it. I won't let anger direct me. Jake has a good plan. I'll go with that. At least for now. "I love you, Izzy," I say softly.

"I love you too, Ty. I love you so much it hurts."

"Take good care of yourself and Christopher, okay?"

"You take care of yourself, okay."

"I'm fine."

"And the horses. How are they?"

I close my eyes, the pain like a physical thing in my body. Let the wind bring the ashes, Tyson. Let the wind do the job. "A foal was born yesterday," I say softly.

"Oh my God, really? How cute. I can't wait to start a new life with you, Tyson."

"Me either."

"Oh dear, your son smells like he needs a diaper change."

"You got to go. All right. Some people will be coming around later. If you need to buy anything just tell them. I'll call back tonight."

"Okay, my darling. Take good care of yourself. Nothing is worth it when you're not around."

I say goodbye, put the receiver back into its cradle, and go out into the reception. Jake is propped up against the edge of his secretary's desk and he is talking on his cellphone. When he senses my presence, he turns around. He straightens and ends his call.

"Come on. Looks like the first person you'll be meeting is my mother."

I hang back. "Is that a good idea?"

"Well, she wants to meet you."

As we go down the elevator, I turn to him. "What's your mother like?"

"She's a true gypsy. Fiercely loyal and devoted to her family."

"Did she sound hurt or mad when you told her about me?"

"Strangely, she was very calm about it. I was planning on telling her last. I wanted you to meet our brothers first. Shane was at her house when I called him and she absolutely insisted on meeting you."

Jake unlocks the latest model Jaguar and I get into the passenger side.

"You said Tony butchered your horses. Do you work with horses?"

"Yes, I breed them."

He frowns. "Ah, so you're that famous horse breeder. A friend of mine bought a horse off you once for me. About three years ago. Her name is Millie."

"You bought Millie?"

"Yeah, she's in my stables right now."

"But the paperwork said it was going to a guy called Tom Watson …"

He grins. "Yeah, the first rule of good business. Never *seem* to buy or own anything."

# TYSON

I never thought I'd say it, but I like Jake. I know instinctively that I am seeing a side of him that he only reserves for his family. Other people no doubt see that cold-eyed man I saw in the club all those years ago. He never asks about my mother, but I know that one day I will tell him. He tells me about Shane and Dom and my half-sister Layla. He also suggests a road trip with his brothers. My chest feels warm and there is a lump in my throat when he says that. It seems that even though I thought I hated them, all I really wanted to was to be reunited with them. To know them. To call them my family. To fill the empty void after so many years without.

He stops the car outside a neat little house with a sweet garden in front. There are colorful gnomes in the garden and lace curtains in the windows.

"I'd love to get her into a better house, but she wants to live here," Jake says.

He has his own key and takes me through the house. I've

been in this kind of house before. Every proud gypsy woman lives in such sparkling cleanliness. I used to be surprised by how many hours a day a gypsy woman spends cleaning her house.

Jake takes me into the kitchen. A woman is rolling out a sheet of dough. She looks up when we enter, then goes back to rolling her dough. She's broader than when I last saw her, and her hair is now peppered with grey. How changed she is from the smiling woman I saw from across the field all those years ago. There are lines on her face. She has known sorrow and pain in her life.

"This is Tyson, Ma. Tyson this is my mother, Mara."

She carries on rolling her dough. "Yes. This is Tyson. Come and sit down, son."

I glance at Jake. He shrugs. His mother puts her rolling pin down and looks at me. There is no expression on her face.

"Do you want me to stay, Ma?" Jake asks.

"No," she says, her eyes never leaving mine. "We'll be just fine. Your sister is in the garden. She was hoping to talk to you."

"Right," he says. He looks at me. "Right," he says again. And it's funny to see this man who controls large swaths of London's underworld get flustered by a woman. He hesitates for another second before he turns and walks out of the back door. Through the window, I can see a woman. She is wearing a sun hat and digging in the ground. Layla. My half-sister.

"I'm not going to apologize for my mother," I say.

She dusts her hands and wipes them on her apron. "Would you like some tea?"

"No thanks," I say.

She moves towards the cupboard and brings out a bottle of sherry. "How about this then?"

I hate sherry, but I can see she is trying her best to be civil so I nod. I watch her pour the amber liquid into two glasses. She lifts one glass to her lips and downs it in one quick swallow. My eyes widen. She brings the other glass to me. I take a small sip. Ugh.

"Have a seat," she says, and we sit opposite each other across the wooden table.

"Do you carry a picture of her?"

At first, I do nothing. Then, I nod.

"Will you show it to me?"

I have never shown anyone my mother's picture. Showing it to this woman feels wrong. She is the enemy, my mother's greatest rival. Because of her my mother died. Then I remember the butterfly and the sense of peace and forgiveness I felt when it landed on my hand.

I'm done hating this woman and her family. I can see that they are good people. And I'm definitely done feeling ashamed for my mother. My mother did nothing wrong. She fell in love with the wrong man. If anyone should be ashamed it should be my father. He cheated on this good woman and ruined my mother's life. I reach into my pocket for my wallet. I open it and slide it along the table surface.

She picks it up and looks at the photo. She keeps her face

blank as she examines the picture. Then she looks up at me. "She was very beautiful."

"Yes, she was," I whisper. At that moment, all the years since my mother's death become dust. I feel as if I am twelve again. Just a kid, lost and afraid, but determined to protect my mother's memory no matter what. I clench my jaw.

"You will stay for dinner with us, won't you?"

I hesitate. Even though my body yearns to accept, a small slice of me knows I can't be part of her family. It would be the ultimate betrayal. I think of my mother's sweet face. How she never bore any ill will towards my father. She was just a sad person. "I wasn't trying to find a home here. I shouldn't be here."

She smiles slowly. "There isn't a grain of dust in this universe that is in the wrong place. You are exactly where you should be."

I stare at her and she nods.

"You want me to be here?"

"Many, many years ago, I went to see a fortune-teller and she told me a strange thing. She told me I had five children. I told her I only had four, but she said, no, I had five. She was very definite about it. For a while I thought I would have another child, but the years passed and I never forgot that she didn't say you will have five children. She said you have five children. You were that fifth child, and I've been waiting for you to turn up all this while."

The breath leaves my body in a rush. "I'm sorry," I tell her.

"For what?"

"I ruined your perfect memories of your husband."

She smiles slowly. The smile is not sad or resentful. It is beautiful. It lights up her face and makes her look ten years younger. "What have you ruined, my child? You have given my grandchildren another uncle, and my children another brother. My daughter always wanted to have more siblings. Now she has a wish. I can't wait to meet my new grandchild."

# TYSON

There was a time when CCTV camera images were grainy and low quality. What Jake's contact gives us to watch is HD standard. Fuck, I can even see the liver spots on the Judge's hands. With surround sound and a massive TV mounted to the wall, it's almost like we're there in the action.

I sit back against the sofa in Jake's dim media room and watch the bizarre sight playing out on the screen. It's a sex dungeon, an S&M club. The walls are covered in black vinyl. In the center of the room is a broad steel table, and on it is a very naked Judge Jackson lying face down.

I rest my chin in my palms as a tall, statuesque, buxom and mature woman dressed in black leather from head to toe, presumably Evanna, walks into the frame, dragging a riding crop along the judge's loose, lily-white ass cheeks.

"Turn around, you are such a worthless piece of shit. Such a loser. Look at that tiny penis. It's disgusting. Which woman would want to touch that? No wonder you have to come here and pay me to get off." My eyebrows rise, but the judge is loving it.

"Evanna knows she is playing for the camera so it should get much better," Jake assures me.

And he wasn't kidding.

The man's got a serious kink problem. He gets flogged mercilessly, then he is asked to get dressed in a woman's bra and diapers and forced to crawl across the floor on his hands and knees before he's allowed to clean her thigh-high boots by licking them. It's not a pretty picture.

To each their own and all that, but hell, how anyone can pay for this shit, let alone love it, but the way his little red cock was hanging stiff and erect between his legs the whole time is a revelation of how aroused he was.

The judge continues to humiliate himself. "Please," he whimpers, begging for the honor of drinking her piss.

"You've been a good boy so today you won't have to drink it from a glass. Today, as a special treat I'll piss straight into your mouth."

He practically salivates while Jake starts laughing next to me. I'm not sure whether I should laugh or wash my eyeballs at the sight of this old guy greedily squatting between her legs and gulping down her piss.

"Holy shit," I marvel when she makes him ram a huge purple dildo up his own ass as punishment for accidentally touching her above the knee while he was drinking her piss. Apparently, that's very verboten. The camera catches it all.

Jake clicks the video off. "That'll do. We'll take this to him and remind him of all the naughty things he did today at lunch time. Unless he takes his son to task this is going to be posted online and sent off to the newspapers." Jake laughs. "He ought to know enough about discipline by now, don't you think?"

"This is preposterous. My son is a fine, upstanding citizen. He runs a clean show. How dare you come in here and threaten me? I know all about you, Jake Eden. You can pretend to be a businessman, but you're nothing but a two-bit crook. Get out of my chambers." The judge, now clad in a dark robe splutters. He raises an arm and points to the door. "I mean it. Out, both of you."

"Chambers?" Jake asks, leaning against a bookcase full of thick, leather-bound books. "Makes a change from dungeons."

The old man's pale skin goes a shade paler as he blinks rapidly. "What?"

"You heard me."

"This is insane. I don't know what either of you are talking about!" I'm afraid the old man's about to have a heart attack. He's sweating profusely.

I drop the USB stick on his mahogany table. "Your honor," I say, folding my arms. "Everything you did at lunchtime is on there."

"Lunchtime?" he sputters breathlessly, staring at the object on his table as if it is a poisonous snake. He looks like is on the brink of a stroke now. If he drops dead, we're fucked.

Men like him surprise me. What do they expect? That one day they won't be compromised?

"Your entire session with Evanna is on there."

"What do you mean?" he asks slowly, even though he knows exactly what I'm saying. If I wasn't so twisted up about my horses, I would feel bad for the old guy. We all have our weaknesses. He just can't get what he needs from the woman he's with.

His eyes fly up to us. He's not ready to give in yet.

"Imagine what it would do to your reputation if it went public," I suggest in a low voice. "Imagine what that would do to your wife."

"And your children," Jake adds.

"Or your high-flying friends," I continue.

His hands ball into fists. "All right, all right. Enough. What do you want from me, you scum?"

"Funny word, coming from a man who can only reach completion while licking a woman's boots," Jake says.

"What do you want? Say your piece and get out of here," he says coldly. This is a very different man indeed from the groveling submissive we saw on the screen.

"Tell your son to lay off my woman and my son," I clarify. "She made the mistake of getting mixed-up with him, but now he won't let her go. I need you to make sure he backs off her. Be grateful that I'm giving you this opportunity because what he's done is enough to get him killed."

"I can't control—"

I hold my hand up. "I don't give a shit how you do it, I just want it done. Threaten to stop turning a blind eye to his activities if you have to. Suggest one of his prior cases be reopened. Call the fucking police on him. I don't care. Just make it happen, and today."

"Or we'll release the footage," Jake murmurs.

"We're not unreasonable. We just need justice. Your son sent around his men and slaughtered a stable full of my prize winning horses. I fucking loved those animals."

His eyes widen with surprise.

"That's right, this is the kind of thing your son does. He kills defenseless animals because he can't get the woman he wants."

His back straightens. He knows his son is no good, but he doesn't care. No matter what that's his son and he'll stand by him.

Any pity I felt for him flees. "If you don't make him under-stand that the woman and the boy don't belong to him, I will release the video online and to all the major newspapers. The British press love juicy debauched stories about our moral, upright judiciary. So no doubt someone will want to print this story. To be clear: I don't want to see or hear from your son or any of his goons again. Understood?"

"Understood," he says tightly. "Now please leave. I never want to see either of you again."

"Yeah, well, I've already seen much more of you than I ever wanted to," Jake slings back.

Judge Jackson stares at us thin-lipped and resentful. It's blackmail after all.

As we turn toward the door, I remember something else. "Oh, one more thing."

"What?" he snaps.

"Since you never taught your son how to treat a woman, I'll have to teach him myself. Just wanted to give you a heads up that I expect no consequences for doing so," I inform him.

He narrows his eyes. "What are you talking about?

"I'm going to give your son the kicking he deserves."

He takes a deep breath and looks as if he would like to say something horrible to me, but all he says is, "Fine. Do what you must, but don't land him in hospital."

"Shame you didn't introduce him to Evanna. A good flogging might've straightened him out years ago," Jake says with a laugh as we leave to find Tony Jackson.

them looks downright dangerous with a scar that runs right down his face. I look into Jake's eyes and all the friendliness and warmth I saw ever since I met him in his office have been wiped out. There, in front of me, stands that ruthless, illusive gangster I saw in the club all those years ago.

Tony stalls and looks around him. His men are watching. It's crazy as hell, but even his own men will not defy Jake. I see Tony clench his fists with frustration. This is not the way he normally does business. His way is to send his henchmen to do his dirty work for him while he plays the big-I-am by hitting women. He already knows he can't fight me. I took care of the three brain-dead dickheads he sent to my house last night.

"Who the hell do you think you are coming into my territory? You want to start a fucking war?" he asks Jake aggressively, blood streaming down his chin.

Jake shakes his head calmly. "Nope. This is my little brother and I'm here to keep it fair."

He frowns. "Your brother?"

"Aye, that's what I said," Jake says with a nod.

"Well, your little brother needs to be taught a lesson. He took my woman."

"She was his woman before she was yours. Christopher is his," Jake's voice rings out in the still space.

"Nah. Finders keepers. She's my woman now and he can fuck off if he thinks I'm giving up what's mine. He can have the brat though."

"You want her. Fight for her then," I challenge.

"I don't fight pussies," he sneers.

"No? That's not what I've been told."

"Fuck what you've heard." He looks me up and down, a disgusted, ugly expression on his face. "I won't fight you, and I'm not giving her up. What're you gonna do?"

I answer with a straight powerful jab, this time on his nose. His head jerks back and the satisfying crack does me good.

"My nose," he howls, clutching it as blood pours from between his fingers.

I make a beckoning movement with the fingers of my right hand. I'm not finished. Not by a long shot.

With a growl full of pain and humiliation, he tries to take me down with a left hook, but I see it coming a mile off and duck. Using my hunched position to my advantage, I sink three, four, five good slugs into his ribs as he reels back helplessly. Groaning he doubles over. I use his own momentum against him and shove his head further down as I bring my knee up sharp and hard. Something else cracks in his face, maybe his cheekbone and he screams like a girl. I don't care. I wish I could break his whole fucking face.

He falls to the floor in a daze, and I kick him in the ribs, the same place I've already punched him. Where he hurt Izzy. He shouts to his men to help him. Not one person moves.

"You want to know who I am? I'm Christopher's father, that's who." Another kick. "And Izzy's man." And another. "Do you understand who I am now?" Kick, kick, I slam my boot repeatedly into his midriff. Begging for mercy he rolls onto his side, away from me, and curls into a ball. I continue kicking his back, hitting his kidneys as hard as I can. Let him piss blood for a while. I'm sure he's done worse to her.

"Enough! Enough!" he blubbers, snot and blood running down his face.

"Not such a tough man when you're not beating up a woman, are you?" I roll him over onto his back. He cowers up at me. "Not so tough when another man uses his fists on you, huh?"

I haul him to his feet. He's a big man, but I'm bigger, and I have all the fury and rage in me. And love. Love for her. My Izzy.

"She's my woman," I spit in his bloody, bruised face. "Mine, motherfucker." He gasps for breath. "If you ever, ever come within a mile of her or my son again, I swear I'll fucking tear you from limb to limb. Do you understand?"

He doesn't answer, his eyes are rolling in his head. Just looks down at the fists which are holding him up.

"Answer me," I snarl. "Oh, and you should know that I've already paid a visit to your father." His good eye goes wide. "Don't worry. I didn't hurt him. But I did manage to convince him to let you fight your own battles on this matter. So. Let me ask you again. Do you understand that I will kill you if you ever come within a mile of Isabelle or Christopher or Izzy's mum again? You or any of your friends?"

He takes a deep, shuddery breath before nodding his head.

"Good." I cock my right arm back and deliver the killer blow to his jaw, shutting off his lights. He is unconscious before he hits the floor.

I look around again before brushing myself off. I walk up to Jake and we leave the pub. No one moves or says anything. As Jake and his men come out its pandemonium inside the pub.

Jake smiles at me. "For a horse-breeder that was an impressive show."

I smile at him. "Thanks, Jake."

"No need to thank me. We're family."

We walk together to the car.

"Where next?" he asks as we slide into our seats.

"Let's go get my family," I say with a grin.

# TYSON

"That's it?" Izzy's eyes are wide with a mixture of disbelief and hope as she searches my face for the truth. "It's really over?"

"Over and done, for good and for all," I promise.

"He gave up just like that?" she asks incredulously.

"Well, he needed a bit of persuasion."

"What kind of persuasion?"

"The kind he uses on you."

Her eyes widen.

"It's safe to say he will not be bothering you ever again."

"How can you be so sure?" she asks, chewing her lip worriedly.

"I'm sure. We'll just leave it at that."

"Oh, no." She cups the side of my face with her hand. "You didn't kill him, did you?"

"Not yet."

"That's not even funny."

"All right. I won't lie. I wanted to, but I didn't. He's still very much alive. Just a bit … unconscious when I left him. He'll heal up, just like you will." I touch her face, then let my hands gently find her waist. "He won't hurt you anymore. Ever, ever again. I already got confirmation from his father that he'll keep him in check for me."

She looks at me with narrowed eyes. "Why would he do that? He adores Tony. Tony can do no wrong in his eyes."

"Believe me," I add with a rueful smile, "it's in his best interest for him to keep him away from my woman."

She shakes her head. "I don't know what to think about all this. It's all too much to take in at once. I'm struggling to get it through my head that he would stay away because of a beating. If I know him he will be itching to take his revenge."

"Take it one day at a time," I murmur, kissing her forehead, then the tip of her nose. "We're all set now."

Her eyes swim with tears. "You're my knight in shining armor"

Her mother enters the room with baby Christopher on her hip.

"Mom," she says. "It's over."

Her mother looks at me, her mouth agape.

"Can I?" I ask, suddenly choked up, holding my arms out for my son. She moves forward and stands in front of me.

For the first time in my life I look into my son's eyes. His eyes are blue, but a different shade than mine, deeper and with a starburst in them. I smile at him and he gives me a big grin. His teeth are tiny and his gums a clean pink.

"Da, da," he cries.

I hold out both my hands in front of him and he raises both his arms and wriggles his body to get out of his grandmother's grip.

I grab him around his solid body and hold him to my chest, marveling at the feel of his strong, sturdy little body. His skin is so soft. His blue eyes look straight into mine, and I'm hooked.

I hear the sound of Izzy crying softly with joy as I touch my lips to the side of his head. I whisper in his little ear, "I'm your daddy, Christopher."

I drive them back to Suffolk, but as soon as we enter the driveway I feel sick. I can't never again live here. Not without my horses. I stop the car and turn around.

"Why are we turning around?" Izzy asks.

"We'll stay in a hotel tonight, okay?"

"Oh, okay," she says uncertainly. "But I really wanted to see your horses."

My hands clench on the steering wheel. Later tonight I'll tell her about my horses, but right now, I can't deal with the emotions. When I was running on autopilot I was numb, but now that the protective numbness is gone, the loss is indescribable. We drive to a hotel and check in. Her mother goes to her room, which is next door to ours, and the staff bring in a cot for Christopher. Very gently, I lower him into his cot. We stand next to each other looking down at him.

"We're so lucky, aren't we?"

I turn to look at her. "I'm the luckiest man on earth."

I pull her along until we are standing next to the wall. As gently as I can, I start to undress her. She clasps my hands.

"I don't look so good," she says.

"You'll be beautiful when you're big with my next child, when you're old and full of wrinkles, when you're sick, when you put on weight, or lose weight. To me you'll always be the woman who turned my brain to jelly. The most beautiful woman on earth. Always perfect."

Her mouth forms an O.

"Now, let me see what is mine."

Her hands drop away. I take off her top. Her bra. Her shoes. Her trousers. Her panties. Her body is black and blue and yellow. My mind takes a picture of her like this because I will never again see her this way. My mouth finds her nipple. It's pink and it belongs in my mouth. I swirl my tongue around it, the ache for her astonishing. I need to lose myself completely in this woman.

"Tyson," she gasps.

I suck the bud and it hardens in my mouth. I let my lips travel across to her other breast and enclose that nipple inside my wet, hot mouth. Her body arches sensuously. I look into her eyes as my mouth trails down to her stomach, gently licking at the swollen discolored flesh I find on my way. I travel down past her hips to the insides of her thighs. As my tongue skims the delicate skin she draws her breath sharply. I trap her legs with my hands and press my mouth against her pussy.

"You're so fucking wet, baby," I growl.

Her hips move, asking for more. "I want you inside me," she whispers.

"I'll be inside you soon enough." Licking her sweet slit gently, I massage her clit with my thumb. My eyes swivel up and lock on hers. She is trying not to moan too loudly. Each time my tongue drags across her clit or swirls around it she shudders. Her eyelids flutter when I slip two fingers inside her hot folds.

"Ahhh …" she groans.

I hate that she has to control herself. I want the whole goddamn world to know that only I can make her sound like that. I lift her right leg and drape it over my shoulder so her pussy is splayed open for me. It is dripping, the little hole pulsating with excitement. I grasp her thigh so she cannot move at all.

Then, without any warning, I bury my head in her pussy and fucking devour her. Fuck, it feels like I haven't eaten her pussy in ages. Plunging my tongue deeper and deeper, I lick the sweet taste from the inside of her walls, savoring the honeyed flavor. It's addictive. My tongue is going to be in this pussy as often as it can. Her hands drop to my head and she grabs fistfuls of my hair. I take her clit in a deep kiss, sucking and nibbling. I want her to cum on my tongue. Her pussy clenches and throbs against my mouth as I bring her to an orgasm.

I place soft kisses on her pussy as she comes down from her high. She touches my face gently. "Holy fuck, Tyson. That was so beautiful. Thank you."

My cock is straining and so hard, it hurts. "I want to come inside you. I want to fill you with my cum." The truth is like an animal I want to mark her. I want to wash away all traces of him. I want to own her pussy.

She nods. I stand up and take her to the edge of the bed. I remove my clothes quickly then I sit on the edge of the bed. Tenderly, I pull her so she is sitting astride my thighs.

"I want you to ride me until I come inside you. I want to see you grind on me."

"Yes," she moans, staring at my cock. She is so turned on her clit is protruding out of its hood.

I position her entrance on my thick cock and push her shoulders down, and watch her sink onto my cock. I watch her pussy swallow my cock inch by inch. The further she slips down the shaft the more she moans. When she finally reaches the root, and she is fully impaled, she stops and allows her body to adjust to my size.

"Ride me, Izzy. Fucking ride me until I fill your sweet pussy up with my cum."

She lifts herself and drops down on my shaft, but I see her wince with pain so I hold on to her thighs and lift and drop her along my shaft. Over and over.

"Oh Tyyyy …" she gasps hoarsely. "You feel so good. I'm about to come."

"Not yet," I growl, but she can't stop. Her orgasm has already started. Her pussy clenches around my cock. I feel the tight tension build in my balls and rise up my shaft and I start to come with her. Her body falls forward. Her breath is warm, heavy and content. I feel the hot spurts shoot into her, and her pussy milks my cock beautifully.

This pussy is mine. Forever.

# TYSON

I sit in Jake's living room watching the happy Christmas scene before me. The whole Eden clan is here. Mara, Dom, Shane, Layla, their spouses, their children, their pets. Never once have I imagined I would ever be part of such a big and wonderful family. That I would be embraced by all these people. Sincerely, and with open hearts and joy, as if I am a gift to the family.

My old life seems like a pale dream now.

I even left Suffolk. It tore me, because I have so many beautiful memories of it, but I couldn't get past that terrible night. I was haunted by their bloodied bodies, their great gasping breaths.

I couldn't even go back for my belongings.

But out of the ashes a new opportunity presented itself. Jake had a large piece of land near his property, and he wanted to give it to me, but I refused. I don't need charity when I am already so blessed. I bought it from him instead. So now I live half an hour from the rest of the family. Ralph moved down with me and I started my stables again. Other than Phoenix, I only own a few horses now, but I'm not in a hurry. I'll wait for the right horses. The ones that I feel in my blood are mine.

Sometimes I still dream of Rubina and Fey, and all the wonderful animals that perished that night. I dream I'm riding them across open grassy plains. The world we are in is vivid. Their feet almost don't touch the ground. We travel the ground as one beast. I know I will meet them again. Real love never dies. My mother is not truly dead. At my lowest hour, she came to me.

I watch Lily, Jake's wife, say something to Izzy that makes her laugh. I stare at the way her blonde hair glints like the finest spun gold. She turns her head suddenly towards me and smiles. Instantly, my heart swells in my chest. Life is so sweet sometimes it scares me. No one can be this lucky. I down my whiskey and stand up. I walk out of the French doors into the cold, dry night. I sniff the air. There'll be snow by tomorrow. The kids will get their white Christmas after all.

I walk over to a bench under a pergola covered by a creeper. I pull my cigarette pack from my shirt pocket and tap out a cigarette. Lighting it, I draw deeply. Hot smoke fills my lungs. I exhale and clouds of white smoke spiral into the still air.

This is my last cigarette. I'm giving it up after this one. It's Layla's fault. Her enthusiasm for organic food and healthy stuff is infectious. Well, it didn't infect me, but Izzy has become one of her 'subjects'. I guess they have a point. Only a fool would buy a box carrying the most disgusting pictures of rotting lungs and undernourished premature babies. I guess I didn't care if I lived a long time, or not before. I do now. I want to stay with Izzy for as long as I can. So I'm giving up smoking as a Christmas present to her.

I hear a noise by the door and turn my head. Jake comes and sits next to me.

"This is my last cigarette," I tell him.

"I'll have one with you."

I look at him, surprised. "I didn't know you smoked."

"I don't, at least not anymore, but I can't let you smoke your last cigarette alone."

I light his cigarette for him and watch him inhale deeply.

"Funny thing," he says. "I always think it's going to taste better than it actually does."

"Hmmm."

For a few seconds neither of us speak.

"Revenge is a double-edged sword," he says softly.

I know instantly what he is talking about. He's referring to Tony's death.

"I didn't do it for revenge. If I had I would have chosen a slow painful death. He had it easy."

"What did you do it for?"

"I did it because men like him shouldn't exist in society. They poison everything they touch. If they cannot be put away because their fathers are powerful judges then they should be taken out."

"How did you do it?"

I shrug. "I know a guy who used to be in the KGB. It's a chemical that mimics a heart attack. The only evidence is a small puncture mark. They used to deliver it on the point of an umbrella in the street. My method of delivery was a whore."

He nods.

"Tony's death was not a revenge, but for payback for those other three who showed no mercy to my horses, for them there will be revenge."

The door opens again and Jake's oldest daughter, Liliana bursts out of it. She is the cheekiest kid I've ever met in my whole life. True I haven't met many, but I'm pretty certain she is unique.

"Are you smoking, Daddy?" she gasps.

"Not really," Jake says dropping his cigarette and grounding it with his shoe. She climbs into his lap and looks innocently into his face. "You know I'll have to tell Mummy about this, don't you?"

"Then I'll have to tell Mummy you ate three spoons of jam straight from the jar."

She thinks about it for a second. "Is that as bad as smoking five cigarettes?"

"I smoked one cigarette, Liliana. One. But ... you had *three* spoons of jam."

She sucks her lower lip into her mouth and considers her position. "All right. I won't tell if you won't."

"Deal," her father says.

She turns to me, her blue eyes shining. "So, Uncle Tyson, does Aunty Izzy know you're smoking?"

I have to laugh. Like I said, there is just no other child like little Liliana Eden.

# EPILOGUE

## IZZY

*One Year Later*
*https://www.youtube.com/watch?v=N4igzqfVyFI*
*How I love you*

"Christopher Flynn, so help me!" I hate having to get down on my knees while wearing a nice dress and heels, but I can't find Chris's other shoe and we're already running late for our reservation. Under the sofa there's crayons, race cars, but no shoe. "I swear, you're enough to drive an angel to drink!"

"Found it, Mommy!"

Tyson swings Chris over his shoulder and jams the shoe on his little foot while our son laughs and squeals and smacks his palms against his father's back.

"Swing me! Swing me!" he shouts.

Tyson sets him on his feet instead. "Not just now, little man."

He straightens Christopher's clothing out. "You're going to stay at grandma's for the night, remember? Mommy and I have important things to do."

"Kissy things?" Christopher giggles with his hands over his mouth.

"Erm, something like that." Tyson smirks in my general direction, but I can only shake my head and laugh.

"All right you lot. Let's get moving before the restaurant cancels our reservation." Tyson picks up Chris while I carry his little backpack, and the three of us walk out to the car together.

A whole weekend alone. What parent doesn't crave it? We drop Christopher off at my mother's. I can hardly stop looking at Tyson, touching his arm, his knee as he drives the car. I can barely wait to be alone with him.

We fly to Paris by private plane. It's been more than three years since I was here last. I thought I would never come back. The memories would have been too painful. It's a special night and I've gone to a lot of trouble to book Tyson's favorite restaurant and a wonderful hotel. Nothing will stop it from being absolutely perfect.

Except a mix-up at the restaurant.

"I'm sorry, but there seems to have been a mix-up," the maître d' tells us.

"I beg your pardon?" I ask with a sinking heart. "I made this reservation three months ago."

"Yes, madam, I'm sure you did, but it must have been entered into the system incorrectly. I have no record of it here, and we're completely full. Perhaps you canceled it and forgot." He gives us a sympathetic smile before turning his attention to the couple waiting behind us.

I feel like such a fool. I've gone and ruined our anniversary. I look up at Tyson. "I'm so sorry, darling. I don't know what happened. I should have made a second call to confirm."

But Tyson doesn't look perturbed. He just shrugs. That's one of the things I've come to most appreciate about him, the way he usually manages to maintain a good outlook. "This isn't the only restaurant in the city," he says as he helps me out of the door.

"No, but this is your favorite restaurant and I wanted it to be special for you," I wail. I'm so disappointed I feel on the verge of tears.

"True, true." He kisses the side of my neck, then murmurs in my ear, "But you know, my hotel has great room service."

And just like that, three years disappear and it's that night again. We're standing on a sidewalk outside an apartment building, and he's trying like mad to get me back to his hotel. I giggle softly at the memory.

"What about this sixties club I know?" he asks.

"Lead the way, good man," I say leaning against him. It's not quite the night I had in mind, especially not while I'm wearing my sexiest dress, but there's something poetic about going back to the place we first got to know each other all those years ago.

Like magic a waitress finds the only available table as soon as we come in. We settle in the back. The crowd seems younger and rowdier than they did before. Maybe, it's motherhood or maybe I'm older. The waitress is quick to return with our Jamesons. We clink glasses.

"This is where I fell in love with you," Tyson says.

"You did?" I ask, blushing a little. Even after a year of living and raising our son together, he still makes me feel like a giggly schoolgirl. He's the only one who does that to me.

"Oh, for sure. You were the most beautiful girl I had ever seen, and the way you moved. I was hiding my erection the whole night."

"I felt it, too," I admit, playing with my glass, smiling to myself. "I was worried nothing would come of it, but I hoped. I really did hope."

"I told myself I was crazy to care so much about a girl I'd only just met, but I couldn't help myself. You were air. I needed to be inside you."

"Me, too," I whisper, looking deep into those familiar eyes and knowing I would never get tired of looking into them. I've never been so happy. Not just now, either, but always. The last year has felt like one long happy dream. Just one day after another that I never want it to end.

"I need to ask you something."

"What?"

He reaches into his pocket, and suddenly I know. That's the one thing I've been wishing for all this time. Even though I don't care a thing about society and what a family "should" look like, I've been wanting to marry him. Wishing he would want the same thing. Thinking he might, but knowing how busy he's been with his horses.

"Oh my God," I whisper, covering my mouth with my hands.

"You had to know something big was coming tonight," he whispers, grinning like mad.

"I didn't dare think about it. I didn't want to be disappointed."

His laughter rings out loud and clear, even over the noise all around us. "I have a confession to make," he murmurs.

"What?" I can hardly breathe.

"I canceled your dinner reservation."

"You what?" I gasp.

He nods, grinning that wicked little grin I see on his son whenever he knows he's done something naughty. "I wanted it to be here, because this place is special for us. We can always go to that restaurant, but this is where we first fell in love. Isn't it?"

"Yes. It is. It's perfect."

"You're perfect. So, Isabella Faraday will you marry me." He opens the box but I don't look at the ring. I'm sure it's beautiful, probably much bigger than anything I would pick out for myself. Instead, I look at him. Beautiful him. He's given me everything I could ever want—love, joy, security, comfort, adventure, a family. And we've only just begun.

"What do you say? Make it official?" he asks.

"Of course, the answer is yes, yes, yes," I choke out before I throw my arms around his neck and squeeze the life out of him. Yes, I want to be his wife. I want to be his forever. I want to have more of his children and fill our home with laughter and love and yes, the occasional fight—but we'll always go back to love. We always do.

"Thank you," I whisper in his ear as my eyes fill with tears of happiness.

"For what?"

"For being my real life hero."

He pulls me away from him and looks at me with the sweetest smile on his handsome face before sealing our engagement with a kiss.

"Chris was right," I laugh as Tyson slides the lovely diamond and platinum ring on my finger.

"About what?"

"About there being a lot of kissy things happening tonight."

# LILIANA EDEN

## A Few Years Later

I look at the grubby boy. He is tall and broad with fierce black eyes and straight black hair. He must be at least a couple of years older than me. I think he's the son of one of the travelling gypsies. His father did some work for my father. He is standing in the garden. His clothes are dirty and his hands are grubby, but for some strange reason I don't understand why I feel drawn to him. I decide to walk up to him and offer him some food.

"What's your name?" I ask.

"None of your business," he says rudely.

"What a rude little boy you are," I say scornfully. "I only came over to see if you are hungry."

"I'm not hungry. I don't need your charity."

I put my hands on my hips feeling angry at his rudeness. "I was only trying to be nice."

His eyes flash. "You want to be nice?"

I look at him, confused. "Well, I did. I'm not sure I want to anymore."

"Then piss off."

I gasp. I don't know why I didn't just walk away and tell Daddy. "Why are you being so rude?"

"Why are you being such a pest?"

"All right I want to be nice. What do you want?"

Suddenly he grabs me and kisses me on the mouth! I am too surprised to resist. His mouth is firm and forceful and hot. Something flutters in my belly. Then he lifts his head and looks into my eyes. I can't look away. I'm too astonished.

"Liliana Eden, I'm going to marry you one day," he declared, before striding away.

I touch my lips. They are still tingling. He kissed me. Ewww … Yuck. The rude boy kissed me! I run towards our house as fast as I can. I burst in through the door and burst into the kitchen, both Mommy and Daddy are there. "A boy kissed me," I announce breathlessly.

"What?" Daddy shouts and jumps up, his face dark with fury.

Mommy grabs hold of his wrist. "She's only eleven, Jake. It doesn't mean anything."

"Fuck it doesn't." Daddy swears furiously as strides out of the house.

I watch him march up to the boy's father. They talk, Daddy gesturing angrily. The man calls his son and slaps him upside the head. The boy says nothing. He just turns his head and looks at me through the window. There is no smile on his face. He just stares at me until his father slaps him again and pulls him away.

I touch my lips. They are still tingling. I wish I had not told Daddy about him.

And the Eden saga continues … :-)

COMING SOON...

EXTRACT

## BLACKMAILED BY THE BEAST

"**M**adison."

I freeze. The street below my window ceases to exist.

Thorne Drakos?

No. No. No. It can't be him. And yet, I would recognize that voice anywhere. I hear the click of my office door closing and his footsteps coming closer. Taking a deep breath, I close my eyes. The deep rumble of his voice is bittersweet.

'Hello, Madison,' he whispers close to my ear. His energy surrounds me. I greedily drag in the scent of his aftershave, leather, pine forests, and the ocean. Oh, god. How I have missed him. These last two years without seeing him have been hell.

I take a step forward then turn around to face him. For a second my whole body goes cold. His eyes. The gray orbs are as frozen as the most inhospitable winter lake. He looks at me expressionlessly. The breath I was holding escapes in a rush. I force a bright smile. "Hiya." My voice sounds breathy and shaky.

He smiles slowly. A cold smile. Full of danger.

I decide to take the bull by the horns. "I'm sorry I stole from you."

His smile widens. It looks almost friendly except for the hostile wasteland in his eyes. "Are you now?"

"Yes, yes, I am very sorry. I'll make arrangements to pay you back."

His eyebrows rise. "What kind of arrangements would they be?"

"I'll take a loan and I'll pay you back every month. All of it. Every last cent."

"With interest?'

"Of course," I agree instantly.

His eyes glitter. "And the cost of finding you. It is very, very difficult to find a girl who stops using her credit cards, social media, and completely drops off the face of the earth."

"Well, living in the UK is not exactly dropping off the face of the earth."

"Let's just say it is hard to find someone when you're looking for Madison Redmond and they're living under the name of Alison Mountbatten."

I swallow hard. "Yes, I figured a new life was the best way forward."

"Hmmm ..."

"If you tell me how much I owe you I'll make arrangements. I ... er ... have work to finish." I indicate to my desk.

"Um ...We could call it two million even."

My eyes pop. "What? I stol ... took $300,000. You can't be serious! You want two million back?"

He shrugs carelessly. "Interest and costs."

"Interest and costs?" I echo incredulously.

He looks at me expressionlessly.

"You don't even need it. It's just numbers in your bank account."

He takes his phone out of his expensive camel coat. "If you'd rather I alert the proper authorities instead—"

I raise my hand up. "Wait. Just wait a second here. We can work something out. I'll pay it all back. I swear. I will. I just need a bit of time."

"So you can run away."

"I won't run. I promise."

He takes a step closer and I stop breathing. His hand rises up and he runs his finger down my exposed throat. "So soft and so pale," he murmurs as his thumb caresses the skin where a pulse is kicking. "How can I trust a thief and a liar?"

"I give you my word."

He shakes his head slowly. "No, Madison. Your word is not good enough."

To my horror my eyes fill with tears. When I blink they spill down my cheeks. He laughs. "The oldest trick in the book. I should have known you'd stoop to that. Well, Alison Mount-batten, I'm afraid female tears have the opposite effect on me." He bends his head and licks my cheek, his tongue warm and velvety. Then he looks into my widened eyes. "They excite me. You, my little thief, are going to cry for me. A lot."

I did not realize that my hands had flown up. I must have wanted to shove him away, but they are resting on his chest, my fingers spread on the hard muscles. "What do you want from me?" I whisper hoarsely.

"I want you to pay your debt with your body."

I blink with shock. "What do you mean?"

"For one year, you will be my toy. You sleep when I tell you to sleep, you will eat when I tell you to eat, you will spread your legs when I tell you to, you will fuck yourself when I tell you to, you will come when I tell you to. You will sleep in my bed and I will use you when and how I decide to."

"You can't do that to me," I say, stunned.

"Or you can go to prison. You will be very sweet meat in a woman's prison. All this soft, unmarked flesh."

I shudder and he smiles. "See. My cock would be infinitely better, no?"

"Why are you doing this? You could have any woman."

"Because I can. Now strip."